This Fool's Journey
Tarot Tales for Modern Minds

Take an enchanting, out-of-the-box journey through the mysteries of the Tarot Major Arcana.

It has long been said that stories are the most powerful teachers, and Cammy Williams' Tarot Tales join a long and noble tradition as they weave us through personal encounters with each of the Tarot's archetypes. When you've finished the journey, the Fool, the Magician, the Devil, the Moon and all the rest will have transformed from obscure, often frustrating symbols to an invaluable collection of friends, acquaintances and wise, challenging teachers!

This Fool's Journey

Tarot Tales for Modern Minds

Cynthia Campbell Williams

For Petrino~,
The mother of so many
wonderful characters; those written and
those waiting to be written —
Enjoy your journey ♡

**ANGEL
HOUSE**

Published by Angel House Press
A division of Stark House Press
2200 O Street
Eureka, CA 95501, USA
griffinskye3@sbcglobal.net
www.starkhousepress.com

This Fool's Journey, *Tarot Tales for Modern Minds*
copyright © 2011 by Cynthia Campbell Williams

Text set in ITC Leawood Std.
Cover design and book layout by Al Williams
Cover art and book illustrations by
Cynthia Campbell Williams

First Angel House Press Edition: February 2011

0 9 8 7 6 5 4 3 2 1

For my family

ACKNOWLEDGEMENT

To thank each of you individually is too much. I am afraid of omitting names.

Of course I thank you, Mr. Al, for the countless hours we've spent together getting this book ready for publishing. You are my editor, my graphic designer, my cheerleader and my dear heart.

Thank you, Faith, for your beautiful introduction and for your years of mentoring This Fool.

Thank you, too, Greg, for your support and for your willingness to publish this collection.

And thank you, Cole, for thinking his Mom can do awesome things.

My mind scans over the memories of the journeys I have walked with you, the "Unnamed Ones" who are my dear friends, family, soul mates, and teachers. I reflect upon the histories that we have created together and I discover that what I am is because of you.

So thank you, each and every one of you. I love you.

TABLE OF CONTENTS

Foreword 1

The Fool 7

The Moon 11

Justice 21

Judgement 33

Temperance .41

The Wheel 51

The Magician .61

Death 71

The Lovers 79

The Chariot 85

The Universe 97

The Devil 101

The Empress .113

The Tower 121

The Star 133

The Hermit 137

The Emperor .145

Strength 163

The High Priestess 173

The High Priest 181

The Hanged Man 191

The Sun 203

Card Explanations 207

About the Author 211

FOREWORD

After studying the Tarot and using it as a professional psychic for more than 40 years, I would have sworn that I'd encountered every Tarot teaching and interpretation paradigm and technique in the world. As so often happens when you think you know it all, I was wrong. And though I usually hate being wrong, this time it was a real pleasure!

This Fool's Journey breaks with traditional Tarot teaching methods in a completely unique way. There is no question that it will help you build a living, breathing relationship with the Tarot's Major Arcana, which many believe is the definitive map of the soul's evolutionary journey.

For your first clue about how far outside the box Cammy has ventured in her quirky, original approach to understanding the Major Arcana archetypes, look at the table of contents. "What?!?!?" You say … "They're not in order! You can't do that!!"

Which, I'm ashamed to say, was my original thought … until I remembered that living systems - humans included - do not evolve by making lists, getting organized and well supplied, and marching briskly from Point A to Point B to Point C until reaching a destination. This kind of organization and categorization is the function of the human left brain, and it has an important place in living systems … but it is focused on identifying and sustaining those systems, not evolving.

No, we and our fellow creatures and environmental systems, both global and universal, evolve by muddling about, heading off in the wrong direction, having to go back and re-do, ignoring signs, screwing up and at most unexpected moments – making a quantum leap. Evolution is creative, intuitive, original and surprising, and it is the domain of the right brain. Evolution doesn't happen without surprise, and it's the intuitive, mysterious and creative right brain that loves surprises. The left brain does everything it can to avoid them, starting by doing everything in numerical order.

Psychology pioneer Carl Jung, mythologist Joseph Campbell and others agree that the Major Arcana cards of the Tarot represent archetypes. Archetypes inhabit the numinous pool of history, feeling, tradition and creation which Jung named the collective consciousness, and an archetype's true presence literally defies definition or rational understanding. Yet, when we learn to use Tarot cards, we laboriously memorize at least two definitions for each card (upright and reversed). Then we struggle to recognize and understand the traditional symbols depicted on each, as well as mastering its numerological and astrological correspondences. No wonder new students feel overwhelmed, and often spend years putting off the moment when they have to leave their books on the shelf and use the cards as personal or professional tools!

But, as any psychic professional who uses Tarot will tell you, there comes a point when you simply have to chuck all of the left brained props of definitions and numeric and zodiac affiliations into the dustbin, engage your right brain, and step off into the unknown.

That's the moment when you walk up, knock on the door of the nearest Major Arcana archetype, and invite yourself in for coffee. You need only decide it's time, and step aside to let your creative, intuitive right brain can come up with any of a million ways to knock on that door, whether it's meditation, painting, storytelling, or stepping out on the tightrope and doing your first bare-knuckle readings.

Cammy has chosen storytelling as her way to introduce us personally to each Tarot Major Arcana archetype, and she has had the courage to surrender completely to the process. She started where she started, and told each short story, not on a schedule, but when, where and how the story made itself known to her.

Her process is akin to walking a labyrinth, like the one in the Cathedral at Chartres. When you walk any labyrinth, you follow a long, twisted path, with many sharp turns, which, unlike a maze, will take you directly (but not straight!) to the center, with no side trips or dead ends. On the journey, you sometimes are just a step from the center, and then suddenly find yourself back on the outer edge, always dancing back and forth, swirling toward the goal, the center, your center. And once you've reached that center, you've covered all the ground. This is Cammy's storytelling style.

It wasn't until I spent "quality time" with the

Chariot (VII) and then the Emperor (IV) that I fully understood how Cammy's approach could reveal more than a straightforward style, particularly for someone who thinks they already know Tarot. Cammy's Charioteer was far more complex than the one inhabiting my right brain, and seemed more like a fully realized Emperor. I wondered about this until later when I read the Emperor's story ... and learned viscerally that the Charioteer is the fully realized Emperor. He has had time to integrate the influence of the feminine force, the Empress. In the Emperor's story he has just met his mate; the Charioteer has lived with and integrated her, and is fully conscious of her value.

But the full import of what Cammy has done finally sank in after I endured the disaster of The Tower (XVI), then soaked in the healing balm of The Star (XVII) and then finally paid a visit to the Hermit. By the time that old Hermit arrived at my campfire I was parched for his wisdom, ready to listen carefully and quietly to his every subtle word, which I surely would not have been had I not had the arrogant stuffing kicked out of me at The Tower, and then been laid bare and vulnerable by The Star.

And isn't that just how we do our lives, our journeys of spiritual evolution? The first time we encounter the Hermit archetype we're too young and impatient to value his zen-like teachings, his asceticism, his lack of material concerns. Only after life has stomped us a few times are we ready to listen.

4

And here's the final bit of magic which evolves from what Cammy has created.

One of the best ways to understand the Minor Arcana of the Tarot is to look at them as numerological families. The fours of Swords, Pentacles, Wands and Cups are aspects of the Emperor (IV) and Death (XIII = 13 = 1+3 = 4). The tens and ones express the ascending energies of the Magician (I), The Wheel of Fortune (X or 10 = 1+0 – 0) and The Sun (XIX or 19 = 1+9 = 10 = 1).

Your understanding will be so deepened by Cammy's stories, these actual meetings with each archetype, that when, for example, the 5 of Pentacles appears, it jumps up and teaches you that it isn't just about starvation and loss, it's also an invitation for you to face the challenges (5) of our everyday world (Pentacles) and use The Hierophant (V) or High Priest's shamanic teachings to master them.

I promise that what you learn in these stories will infuse every future Tarot encounter with a vivid, living reality which will keep growing to take on a life of its own. That living presence will infuse and inform every card, every reading, every meditation and, in the process, free you to build a real working relationship with Tarot, or deepen one of long standing.

Blessings,

Faith Freewoman
California, November 7, 2010

The Fool

Chapter..0 The Fool

I am an artist—a painter—and I collect tarot cards. I find the cards amazing, beautiful and mysterious. As I hold them, they seem to buzz with ancient power.

Although not a tarot card reader, it excites me to know that each card contains an archetypal energy just waiting to be tapped and understood.

My name is Jude and like I said, I'm a painter. I paint only in oils because I enjoy the rich history of oil painting, the vibrant colors and the fact that they never truly dry even when they appear dry to the touch.

My work is well received and I've created a niche for myself as a visionary artist. My paintings "inspire and open up the imagination, and explore different possibilities of reality." Or so the art critics write.

I enjoy my life and what I do. Currently, I'm taking a break from painting, and simply experiencing life; breathing in inspiration.

The new deck I just opened are all in order. Shuffling them, I study each one individually. The artwork is exceptional and I feel a deep kinship to this artist.

With a psychology background, particularly studying Carl Jung's archetypes and his theory on active imagination, I am particularly drawn to the Major Arcana—the first 21 cards with names such as The Empress, The Devil, Death, and Judgment. I wonder what it would be like to meet these—not really knowing what to call them—different expressions of a way of being? Archetypal forces? I ponder what it would be like to live within the energy that the cards' pictures indicate.

My desire is to understand the essence of each card and make it mine. I look through the deck, separating out the Major Arcana and placing them in a pile. The pile isn't in any particular order and I draw one to contemplate. I'm curious to see what will unfold as I choose one card at a time.

What path will these cards have me take?

The card in my hand is The Moon. My eyes close and I imagine...

Chapter 1 ...The Moon

"And so it begins," Jude thought. She was dressed in white, a flowing robe tossed over white drawstring pants and a loose over-shirt, all in the same fabric. Her feet were bare. Her dark, wavy hair was unbound. She sat stiffly on a chair in a darkened room. It was dusk and the world was quieting, preparing for night.

She sensed a presence at the door, the latch clicked and the Reverend Mother entered. Through the open door came the smells of dinner, the warm bread and soup that Jude had helped prepare. It had been an ordinary day like all the others.

Tonight would be different, a night of choices and change. If she survived the night, she

could never return to what she was now,
a mere child in a chair with unbound hair.

The night had been chosen especially for her.
The Reverend Mother read the stars and
consulted with the High Priestess to find the
night that would support Jude the most on her
journey within.

The Reverend Mother looked at her with an
expression Jude decided was best described as
"inscrutable." She was dressed in a similar
fashion to Jude. Her waistline revealed many
honey cakes and bread. Her inscrutable face
shone with power.

At that moment, the Reverend Mother smiled
and said, "So it begins, my child."

Fearful but trusting, Jude smiled back.

She had known this day would come, why
not today?

"Have you prepared?" The Reverend Mother
asked.

"Yes, Mother," she replied.

"Are you afraid?"

"Yes, Mother."

12

"You are wise, my daughter. Remember, all will be what it will be. If you allow the events to evolve as they transpire, it will go well for you."

"What would happen if I don't?" Jude asked.

The Reverend Mother smiled and reached out to cradle her upraised face. "That is not how you were trained to think, dear one."

With that she reached deep within the folds of her cloak and withdrew a small glass vial, presenting it to Jude.

Jude's heart beat rapidly as she uncorked the vial and drank. Its milky contents had no odor, although it was very bitter. She wiped her hand against her mouth and recorked the vial, handing it back as the Reverend Mother sighed.

Jude stood, feeling small and helpless, engulfed within the warm strength of the Reverend Mother's embrace.

"It won't be long now, child," she said, "Your sisters will be waiting for you on the other side of this night. Remember that All Is Well and to allow the events to transpire as they will."

Then, the Reverend Mother was gone. In the suddenly quiet room, the dinner smells lingered long enough to cause Jude's stomach to growl.

She slowly returned to her chair. Too restless and uneasy to sit still, she crossed over to the window to watch the last colors of the remaining sunset merge with the rising full moon's light.

The door opened behind her. Startled, Jude abruptly turned around. It was only the cat— the one with unusually round, green eyes. "Come outside," purred the cat.

"I am not supposed to leave this room," Jude answered.

"You are also to allow the events to transpire as they will," replied the cat, flicking its tail.

Jude surrendered to what was, whispered to herself that all was well and followed the cat out of the room. The corridor was long, dark and silent. She felt trapped, longing for the open expanse of the outside. The cat trotted ahead of her, its tail held high, to a small side door near the kitchen. Putting a paw on the door, the cat waited for Jude to open it.

The night air was chilly and crisp, but smelled

like summer was just around the corner. The cat led Jude down a garden path and they entered a small enclosure with a bench. Jude sat down, feeling much better being outside. The slanted rays of the rising moon had swallowed the colors, leaving only shimmering silver, grey and blue.

The cat jumped and curled upon Jude's lap, tucking her paws underneath. Without realizing, she stroked its soft fur. The cat rewarded Jude with a comforting purr, making her feel languid and drowsy. "Cat," she asked, "What are you most afraid of?"

"*Nothing*," purred the cat. "What about you?"

Jude thought.

"*Nothing*. I'm afraid of *Nothing*, too," she replied.

The cat purred.

"What is *Nothing*, exactly?" Jude asked the cat.

The cat looked at her with its large green eyes. The pupils were dark and rimmed with green. The cat's eyesight was so much better than Jude's. It was designed for seeing at night. "*Nothing* is that which is not yet something," it answered.

"Why are we afraid of *that*?" Jude wanted to know.

"Because *Nothing* can turn into something and, in the wrong hands, *Nothing* can be a very bad thing, indeed," the cat answered.

Jude shivered and asked. "How does it get to be in the wrong hands?" adding, "I don't like being afraid."

"If you keep your control of *Nothing*," explained the cat, "then, there is nothing but potential and it no longer is a fearful thing." The cat laughed through its whiskers. "Potential is the source for all that you desire. Everything begins with the potential to become something. Potential first, then possibility, and then reality."

Suddenly the cat leapt from Jude's lap, and onto an unsuspecting vole. Jude watched as it toyed with the vole before killing it.

She grimaced.

The cat settled down to eat, relishing the warm flesh it found under the fur and skin.

"So how do I keep my *Potential* for myself?" Jude inquired of the feeding cat.

The cat was silent while finishing its supper.

16

Jude noticed it had left the vole's head and feet and looked away. She turned her gaze to the full moon. It was so bright she would have been able to read if she had a book.

The cat began to wash itself.

"With every belief you have that is not your own," the cat began, "you lose a little bit of your potential. Little by little, it disappears without notice until you are enveloped by others' beliefs and habits. You're left with no more potential. It has all evaporated to feed others' possibilities. It has become others' realities. You are left with *Nothing*, lifeless *Nothing*." A dog or wolf howled. The cat paused mid-cleaning and asked, "More frightening—don't you think—than anything?"

Jude wrapped her arms around herself tightly and nodded. "So, how do I prevent others' beliefs from taking away my potential? From when I was very young, other people have shown me what to do and how to be. Cat, is it too late for me?"

The cat yawned, its tongue curling as cats' tongues do. "Simply ask yourself WHY when a belief comes knocking at your door. If the answer to your WHY is satisfactory, then let the belief in. If it's not, throw the belief out." The cat flexed her paw. "Or kill it. It is what we do. People find cats willful creatures, but that is only because we pick and choose what beliefs we give our potential to."

The cat looked up at Jude sitting on the bench with her arms wrapped tightly around herself. "You do not need to be afraid, Jude," it said. "After all. It's only *Nothing*."

The cat stretched, stood and stretched some more. "I want to go inside now. Will you let me in?" she asked in a quiet purr.

Jude looked at her. The cat looked so beautiful in the moonlight with its round green eyes. "Yes, cat, I believe I will." Jude consented.

She unwrapped her arms, stood and stretched, sucking in a lung-full of the crisp air. Looking around, she appreciated the subtle blues and grays of the moon-shimmered landscape.

Jude smiled, following the cat whose tail stood straight up in the air like a flag. The cat was already halfway to the small door near the kitchen where there would be hot soup, bread and honey cakes.

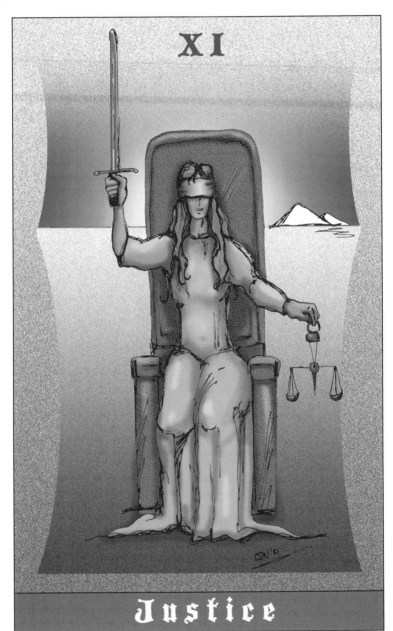

XI

Justice

Chapter 2 ...Justice

There was no lock on the cell door. But then again, Jude thought, where were you going to go in this small, rust-bucket of a space station? Besides, he was in the fourth quadrant of this galaxy with an ID insert that was able to track his every move.   Annoyed, he opened the door and stuck his head out. The corridor was empty, except for lighting panels and the occasional speaker.

Closing the door, Jude slapped the room's speaker panel. As it sputtered to life, he requested water and some sort of protein, he didn't care what kind. The automated voice acknowledged his request. There was already nourishment in the room, but he didn't like what he had found, and there was no liquid labeled "water."

While waiting for his order to arrive, Jude looked out of the small observation window. His hands were clasped behind him and with his legs braced, he stood, head held high. Things could be worse, he supposed. He could have been placed in an inside cell with no windows to see the stars and the incoming ships.

This space station was small and scarred from space debris. He slowly shook his head and wondered to himself how, with all of his skills and training, he had landed in this mess.

Abruptly, Jude turned and sat down in front of a small desk and screen. His captors had suggested that he might like to rescarch relevant topics before he was brought in front of The Counsel. That had made him laugh at the time. Research relevant topics? What relevant topics?

He got up and, in two steps, reached the small cot. "This cell is not going to get any larger by me walking from end to end," he remarked, looking down at the neatly folded uniform lying on the cot. It was a special uniform worn only on certain occasions. Like a visit with The Counsel.

He returned to the window, bringing the desk

chair with him so he could sit and look out. The vast expanse of space had always made him feel at peace and balanced. He deeply inhaled, letting it out slowly, willing himself to relax and think.

It had been during a routine transport job that he had been arrested. His was a small company—just his ship and him—specializing in interplanetary/interdimensional puddle jumps, to deliver supplies. He led a quiet life. He paid his taxes and remained under the radar. He didn't look for trouble and trouble usually never found him and he liked it that way. It was a risky business, especially when he went interdimensional, but his extensive training had taught him the rules. That didn't mean he followed them, though.

He had fired his weapon...on a third dimensional planet...and it was not in self-defense.

It was because of that girl. It would always be that girl.

Jude smiled.

The very first time he met her was by mistake. She was so illuminated that he swore she was from the Fifth. After all, he had been servicing a city of the Fifth, right? It was just beyond the city's perimeter that he had caught a glimpse of her. Or rather, she had first seen him. It was because of a loud gasp of surprise that he had realized she was even there. Maybe he shouldn't have wandered so far outside the perimeter, but the beauty of this particular planet had drawn him and he hadn't gone very far.

There she was, smaller and more petite than the other city dwellers. But she was blond and she glowed with her own inner light, just like a normal Fifth. Her fear had made her flicker a bit and he momentarily lost sight of her. Even though he couldn't see her, he knew she was still there, so he talked, calming her the best he could until she blinked back into Fifth's reality.

After that first meeting, it had continued. Whenever he made his deliveries there, he would look for her. Most of the time, she'd be there waiting, and when she wasn't, he was always surprised by his disappointment. In the beginning, he hadn't thought too much about her unless he had taken a consignment for delivery to her planet.

She told him how connected she felt to him, and that he was one of her Guides. He knew the rules, so he could never prove or disprove her conviction, but it still made him laugh.

24

Rules were rules, but in his mind there was always a way around them, so he bent them just enough to have good conversations with her. He continued to hold her interest by telling her some of the ways he traveled between the planets and the different dimensions. Jude explained to her how the cosmos was constructed in tonal, vibrational dimensions, arranged in interlapping spirals. When you learned the energy signature of a dimension, all you had to do was align with that vibration and you'd be there. Of course it took practice and, along with his ship's technologies, he was able to adapt faster. As a rule one never went below Fifth, however he didn't go into details. Abiding by the rules, he would let her develop her own assumptions.

It turned out that her assumptions had been quite popular on her planet in the Third, where she was actually from. She had written books on the subjects he had shared with her. Eventually, she had earned enough money from her books to allow her to buy the property where they had first met. There, she established a Retreat Center, as that's what she called it. By and by, she met others from the Fifth city. They all knew the rules, but she was persistent. Her inner illumination kept growing brighter, making her all the more beautiful.

He began visiting that Fifth city more often, even when he didn't have reason to go there. The Fifth city, so very near where that girl, now a middle aged woman, lived. On her, middle age looked spectacular, as she was becoming an Elder, a Wise-One, an Elevator. It gave Jude so much pleasure watching her grow in knowledge and understanding. Her glowing was becoming so bright, it wouldn't have surprised him if she occasionally slipped into Seventh or, even on rare occasions, Ninth.

That's when the two men arrived. Without an understanding of the Third's motivations, he didn't really know what they wanted. However, he did know that the girl was frightened, so terrified that he couldn't even see her. All he could do was listen to her cries of distress.

By pure chance he was there, on her planet. It was happenstance that he had been walking into her Retreat Center. Although he was aware of the rules, this was *HER*, and she was afraid for her life. Without thinking, Jude fired his weapon. Twice. Firing blindly, he aimed away from the direction of her cries, but close enough if they had been touching her. He was amazed that he had even hit them.

After he had fired, there had been only silence.

In the stillness, Jude stood with terror in his heart. He wasn't thinking about rules or the repercussions. He was only thinking about *HER* and whether he had killed her. Because he was on Fifth and she had slipped into Third, he couldn't tell. He couldn't see her; and he could no longer hear her.

Anyone living in Fifth knows when a weapon is discharged. It reverberates, sending sickening vibrations out in ever expanding echoes. It didn't take the authorities long to find him, contain him and escort him off-planet where he could do no more damage.

Under the interrogation that followed, the whole story had unfolded. Now he waited in his cell to be summoned by The Counsel. Jude wondered what would arrive first—the summons or the water and protein he had requested.

It was the girl who had introduced him to water and he couldn't get enough of it. He especially liked the kind that bubbled up from deep within the planet.

A tap on the door turned his attention away from the window. A panel in the door slid open to reveal a man dressed in a uniform.

27

It looked very much like the uniform lying on his bed.

"Is it time?" Jude asked.

The man nodded. "I will wait outside for you." he said, pausing for Jude's acknowledgment before closing the door.

Jude quickly washed up before reaching for the uniform. One did *not* keep The Counsel waiting. Feeling the unfamiliar fabric against his skin, he hurriedly slid on the uniform. Upon seeing himself in the mirror, he ran a hand through his long wavy hair, shrugged at his apprehensive expression and walked toward his cell door.

The door opened at his thought. Jude stepped through and joined the man waiting in the corridor.

Silence escorted the two men up to the next level and into The Counsel's Chamber.

The Counsel was an Eleventh. Jude had never met an Eleventh before. He really didn't see much of this one, either, except for a very bright light,that caused him to squint and look away. A Ninth, positioned beside The Counsel, did the transmitting.

"We know your story and are nearly ready to proceed with the Just Edict," the Ninth explained. "Before we commence, however, we feel your need to inquire and you may do so at this time."

Jude swallowed, bowing in gratitude. "How," he stuttered, swallowing again and wishing for something to drink, "How is she?"

"She lives," the Ninth replied, "You did not damage her."

Jude smiled, knowing that he was probably glowing as brightly as she ever did. He didn't care. *She lived!*

"Are you ready to hear the Just Edict?" asked the Ninth.

Jude, still glowing, nodded.

"You know the rules," transmitted the Ninth, "and you have a choice." He paused, receiving more information from the Eleventh. "We give you this choice because it was from your actions that the Third's growth into Fifth and beyond was accelerated. It was your teaching that permitted her to accelerate the growth of others. However, you acted without thought and destroyed two Thirds and damaged the balance for several Fifths."

The Ninth stopped briefly before continuing, "Destroying the Thirds as you did, prevented them from continuing on their path, thus saving them from the negative experiences they were inviting into their lives. And we have taken into account that your motivation was love. The Thirds that you destroyed served their function in deepening your understanding of love which provided a more favorable outcome when they came before The Counsel and were served their Just Edicts."

The Ninth paused again. "These are the choices you have: You may continue as you have been doing with your transportation function. However, you will be restricted from her planet. Or, you may isolate yourself there and remain with the Third, never to travel off-planet again. These are your choices, are you ready to decide?'

Jude thought briefly about his love for the stars. About the openness and expansive freedom he felt traveling among them. However, he could not stop his glowing. Jude grinned. Soon, he would be able to drink water whenever he wanted.

Chapter 3 ...Judgment

Jude woke up with a jolt, sitting straight up in bed even before her eyes opened. Something was exceptionally different, she thought. Not wrong, just...different.

Opening her eyes and pushing the hair from her face, she looked around at the unfamiliar and rather Spartan surroundings—a bed, a chair, a wooden floor, walls devoid of any ornamentation, a window with the shade drawn, all in various shades of creams and whites. The light from the window gave the place a warm feel.

Jude pulled back the yellow blanket and slipped her feet into the slippers waiting there for her. Crossing to the window, she lifted the shade to peer out at...nothing. The world was...blank—just the light—but all very familiar.

"Oh," Jude thought, memory flooding her consciousness. "I've crossed." she said out loud.

She manifested a hand mirror and looked at her last face. She liked this one, she thought. It suited her. Perhaps she'll wear it again sometime. Returning to her bed, she sat down. Closing her eyes, she went within, readying herself. Her mind glided through her recent memories and felt satisfied that all was in order.

It felt good to not be weighted down any more. She was so light! And she had had a good life. That was another good feeling. Things were so different than they used to be. Transitions were easier to make, the deathing experience wasn't as disorienting as it had once been. She'd almost, not quite, but almost realized the reality of Reality before she crossed back over. Hopefully her work had helped cement that into Humankind's collective thoughts.

Jude stretched her mind, connecting up with her Soul Family, felt their joy, felt her eager anticipation of their reunion.

Suddenly they were all there. Together in a meadow with a soft breeze blowing, all looking at one another, touching minds and laughing, flowing and merging, remerging, and sharing experiences. No longer separated, but united—even with the ones still incarnated, although they weren't yet aware of it.

Jude expressed her need to take a break from the incarnation merry-go-round. She decided to be a guide for the next member of the Soul Family who wanted to step into a soul suit to have an experience. Jude had been in several soul suits in succession, and with her recent return, she would be an asset as a guide. They agreed with her.

"It is getting easier," she informed them. "We are so close to ascending to a new spiral. It is very exciting."

One of her Soul Family, still incarnated, agreed. "My dreams are so real. I will wake up and remember this experience, " he said. "I am often confused during my day because I think I've had conversations with people and then realize that I had had them only in my dream-state!"

"Yes!" said another, excitedly. "I would sometimes think my dreams were more real than my everyday reality. Then, when I did cross, I realized that I was right!"

They all shared the humor.

"Isn't it wonderful to cross when you have had a particularly difficult incarnation?" another asked.

"I sometimes would pick a traumatic life just so I could cross and feel the joy of being back," Jude said.

She felt their confusion. "But isn't that the point?" she asked. "Are we not exploring and answering the what-ifs so that we can expand to be more than we were?"

"But to deliberately have a traumatic life," one answered in confusion, "it does not seem right. Pick a traumatic life to see if you can grow from it, to try to keep the oneness even in the face of seeming separation. But, to pick a traumatic life just to feel the joy of being back?"

Jude stilled herself as she felt the others' confusion wash over her.

"That is why I am tired of the wheel," she began... "that game is played out to me. Look at my lives. I have had several where I have regained oneness in the face of separation. I want to express oneness differently now."

36

She paused in front of the silence of the others. They sensed something new, listening intently. "Because we have worn so many soul suits, we forget that Humankind is *not* a series of soul suits. We are created with joy and with joy is how we naturally exist. With joy is how we should be. Within, or without a soul suit. Within or without a created reality. Oh how weary I am of the wheel!" Jude continued, "I want to explore oneness without separation. I wish to step into a soul suit if I want something to eat and then step back out of it. I wish to step into a soul suit if I want to feel the sun on my skin. I wish to step into a soul suit if I want to drive a car or run on a beach. I wish to be free to do these things and to be free to enjoy others doing these things too. Tell me, wouldn't that be much more fun? Think of the wonders we can share and create! Think of the newness—to live in oneness and joy—to delight for eternity."

She couldn't help herself. Feeling the joy of that possibility—-she expanded and burst into thousands of sparkling lights that flickered and danced and shimmered. Gathering back into herself, she waited for the response from her Soul Family.

"But how can that happen?" asked one, a young soul.

"Humankind just has to realize that it only struggles if it wants to struggle," Jude explained. "We need to design our lives to show it to be true. The more of us that do this, the more examples we can set. The more examples we can set, the more that notion will lock itself into Humankinds' collective memory and the sooner the possibility will become a reality."

"Suppose several of us incarnate at the same time with the same objective," said one, "we could hasten the process."

"Even better, " said another, "why don't we merge with those already incarnated and manifest these concepts now? We can by-pass the childhood-to-adulthood experience."

"Oh, I like that!" said the young soul. "I will go!"

"And I will receive you," said one of the dreamers.

"As will I," said another, then another, and another.

It was decided and agreed and arranged and done.

Jude watched with joy as the patterns formed and reformed, spiraling forth into a new path of possibilities.

Chapter 4
...Temperance

"The only thing good about this school," thought Jude, rolling out of bed in the pre-dawn stillness "is the uniforms." It was like wearing pajamas all day and, in fact, he often slept in his. It meant he could sleep just that little bit longer. With a yawn, he splashed water on his face from the basin he set out the night before. He ran his fingers through his unruly mass of hair, slipped his feet into the shoes waiting by the door and exited his dorm room. Knowing he was going to be late because he always was, he took off down the hallway in a shuffling lope, trying to be mindful of the others still asleep behind the doors he was passing.

The shock of the cold morning air woke him fully when he pushed open the front door of the dormitory. Jude broke into a run, heading for the Quad where he could see others already in position and beginning their energy work. He could feel the Master's eyes on him as he found a place in the back row, as far from the Master as possible. He hated the scrutiny and envied the others who could perform the intricate patterns of the energy grids with ease even if the Master was watching. He shot a questioning look at his neighbor who mouthed the word "Mer-ka-ba." Jude smiled back in appreciation, inwardly groaning.

The Mer-ka-ba was one of the simplest grids to learn and one of the most difficult to perfect. It was said that it was the basis from which all the other energy grids came. If a student were to practice only this grid, he could achieve mastery over all the others; mastery, even, over himself.

Jude began by quieting his breath, drawing in the morning's stillness with each lung-full of air. When he felt "ready," he settled himself into the balancing stance—the beginning place for all grids. From this stance he moved into the preliminary movements of the Mer-ka-ba. It was usually here that he would begin to falter, forgetting which grid pattern he was supposed to be doing or moving into a pattern that was only his own and made no sense to others. But this morning he was lucky. This morning, the movements of the Mer-ka-ba came readily to him and he fell into a half-trance as he performed them over and over again, taking pleasure in the feel of the energy gathering and breathing within him. Eyes half-closed and unfocused, he lost awareness of all else except for the simple yet beautiful patterns of the Mer-ka-ba Grid.

Jude came to his senses with a start. He nearly fell, arms windmilling to regain his balance. He looked around to see if anyone else saw him, waiting for the inevitable snicker. His eyes widened as he discovered he was alone....alone save for the Master who was watching him, his eyes crinkling in amusement. Jude could feel his face reddening.

"Master, I-I'm sorry," he stuttered. "I lost track of time."

The Master reached out and touched Jude's shoulder, steadying him. Jude could feel the Master's power from the brief contact. "It happens," replied the Master calmly, "but it was a good lesson for us all." Jude hung his head.

"Why do you show shame?" the Master inquired. "Do you assume that the lessons you show others always come from the negative?"

Jude looked at him briefly and shrugged.

The Master smiled. "Well then, young sir, you will be surprised to know that today, you did everything just right. The harmonics you created reached out and touched us all. It was very beautiful, Jude. It was perfection."

Jude looked at the Master in surprise. "Perfection?" he asked.

"Perfection," the Master confirmed, "and even more of a marvel coming from one such as you."

"Coming from someone who always screws it up, you mean," replied Jude.

The Master chuckled. "Your perceptions of yourself have created a misunderstanding. What *I* mean is you have had so little formal training, yet you have perfected the Mer-ka-ba, a grid that many fail to fully comprehend." He paused before continuing, "In all my years of teaching, Jude, I have never seen it done so well. All of us have benefitted from the harmonics you created...and we thank you."

Jude looked at the Master who smiled quietly back at him and he felt the beginnings of an emotion stirring in his heart. It wasn't pride--although that was an emotion that was long overdue--rather, it was joy and his face radiated with it.

"Jude," the Master began, "I have something to tell you that, until today, I did not feel you were ready to hear. Come, let's sit." He gestured to a nearby bench and the two made their way over to it and sat. It had a beautiful view of the campus grounds and of the ocean beyond. Jude felt soothed as he watched the whitecaps form and then disappear.

"I will not be the Master forever...," the Master said.

"No duh," thought Jude, and he glanced over at the Master.

The Master chuckled, as if reading Jude's mind. "Since the day I became Master I began looking for my successor. I've been seeking for many years and today," he paused to check if Jude were listening, "today I have found him. It is you, Jude," he said quietly.

Jude went rigid, eyes widening. He searched the Master's face. "You must be joking!" he exclaimed. "I'm...I'm... I'm a Nobody! I don't do anything right!" He ran his hands through his hair. "There's no way! I could never be like you!"

The Master smiled. "But you already are like me—or like how I used to be. I noticed you the first day you stepped foot on this campus. Granted, you have a way to go, but never doubt that this is what you will become."

"You don't know me," said Jude stubbornly, "I'm pretty worthless, a total disappointment. Ask anybody." He turned his gaze back to the whitecaps on the horizon, his thoughts in turmoil.

"Not so, Jude, " the Master replied gently, studying the boy's profile, "especially after today. You did not see the awe in the faces of the others when you performed the Mer-ka-ba. You will now see a difference in how you will be treated. And it will take some getting used to, I assure you. And know this, too—the class and I weren't the only ones touched by the harmonics, Jude. The Mer-ka-ba worked its energies upon you, as well. You will see. You are not the same boy who," he glanced at the wrinkled uniform

46

and chuckled, "woke up just in time for their energy work this morning."

"So who am I then?" Jude said to the Master, eyes still following the waves.

"You are my Apprentice, Jude, and it will not be easy."

"Do I have a choice? Can I think about this?" Jude asked. He never liked feeling as if things were happening to him without his control. This was happening fast, too fast. He felt helpless.

"No, you do not have a choice, my son, not now. I am sorry. But you *can* think about it. You can think about it as often as you like."

"What do you mean by 'no choice,' I thought we always had a choice." Jude challenged.

"What you do not realize, Jude—and you will some day—is that you made your choice this morning. You made your choice when you proved to me beyond the shadow of a doubt that on some level, you understand what the Mer-ka-ba Grid is. If you did not, you could not have done what you have done today."

"But I don't want to be a Master-in-training!" Jude retaliated. "I want to be just a kid!"

"And are you enjoying being just a kid?" came the reply. "Aren't you the least bit curious what it would be like to be my Apprentice—to learn all that I know and to gain knowledge even beyond what I know?"

Jude opened his mouth to answer, but the Master held up his hand. "Don't be too hasty in your response, my boy. Never speak empty words that have no thought behind them. Thoughtless words create discordance." The Master rose. "I will leave you now, Jude. Take some time to think about what I've told you. Take the rest of the day because tomorrow it all begins." The Master glanced down at Jude, taking in his scowling, rebellious expression. "And my first assignment to you as my Apprentice, is to think how it felt when you performed the Mer-ka-ba Grid just now." He touched the boy's shoulder and left without a backward glance.

For several moments, Jude remained as he was—rigid, angry, frustrated. But then, despite himself, he began to think about the Grid. He replayed its pattern in his mind.

It did not take long for the joy to return.

Chapter 5 ...The Wheel

Seeing the shade, Jude stopped under the tree. She leaned her back against it, closing her eyes, concentrating on her breath, willing it to slow. It took awhile. But then, she'd been running for some time now.

She opened her eyes and squinted at the heat shimmering on the horizon, blurring the line between land and sky. A ribbon of sweat ran down between her shoulder blades. She pulled her heavy dark hair off her neck, letting the damp dry and cool her.

This morning in the pre-dawn it seemed like a good idea for a walk-a-bout. But then, in the cool and the mess back home, lots of things seemed like a good idea. The walk-a-bout was the easiest one. So, she had gathered the things she would need and took off in a lope, heading West—away from the dawn, into the shadows. She knew better than to run. She knew she would need to save her strength. The ocean was still miles away. But it had felt so good to put as much distance as possible between her self and the sameness that was her home life.

Jude took the pack off her back, opened it, and rummaged around for one of the oranges she had shoved into it. Buried deep, it was still cool to her touch and she hurriedly began to peel it. Pulling off a section, she closed her eyes as she took her first bite, savoring the cool, sweet liquid running down her dry, dusty throat. Pure heaven.

Opening her eyes again, she looked west at the faint ridgeline on the shimmering horizon. Behind the ridge was the beach. Her destination. It was a two-day trek, one she had made many times before.

With a sigh, she shouldered her pack and set off at a walk this time, giving thanks for the shade and the orange. As she walked, she remembered the last time she'd come this way, smiling at the memory. Things had been different then.

She stopped her mind from remembering further. It was best to just let it be. With an effort, Jude changed her thoughts...to the dolphins.

For the past several nights, Jude had been dreaming of dolphins. In the dreams, she was swimming with them and when she woke, the joy she had experienced would linger long into the day. She was grateful for the dreams as they balanced out her waking moments. The dreams were the reason she was heading west.

It wasn't as if her life were bad, it just wasn't good. It revolved around others, and her ideas and her insights never counted. Her suggestions in farm management were scoffed and ridiculed. Yet later, to her quiet amusement, those very suggestions always seemed to find themselves within the routine of the ranch's day-to-day workings. There was no acknowledgment, however, no nod of thanks in her direction. She felt less-than-human and she felt her life was drying up in the heat of the ordinary. Each day was like the last, over and over and over again. She felt beaten down and worn out and she was terrified that if she didn't do something, she would vanish into the sameness and lose her will to live entirely.

She felt old, too, older than her years. She would catch her reflection in a mirror or store window and be surprised at how young she really was.

The trail Jude was on was barely visible, but she knew where she was. She was walking across a high plateau and she could see for miles in all directions. Ahead of her, the ridge was still too far away. She kept walking, letting the rhythm put her in a semi-trance as her thoughts spun around and around in the rut of frustration they had created.

The sun's glare hurt her eyes and she looked down, watching as each footstep produced little puffs of dust. As the day heated up, she reasoned she could stop and find shade, wait for evening. But she couldn't quell the restlessness and the need to walk away from the sameness of her life. She knew of a year-round spring about two miles ahead. Perhaps she would rest a little there, wet the bandanna that she wore around her neck and tie it around her forehead to keep her cooler.

The hours drifted by and soon it was late afternoon. The ridge was much closer and Jude knew she would reach it by nightfall. There was a small sheepherder's cabin, seldom used but well stocked where she could find shelter.

54

That night she dreamed of dolphins, a large pod of them this time.

At dawn, Jude set off again and by late-morning found herself high atop the ridge, gazing at the ocean view. As she made her descent, she lost sight of the ocean when the trail wandered into a steep valley, following a small creek. The heat changed from dry to humid. The air was ripe with scent. The steepness of the path kept her focused and she lost track of time. When she reached the beach—a small cove—she dropped her pack and ran to the water, welcoming its coolness as it cascaded over her legs.

Scanning the bay, her joy at her journey's end was dampened by the absence of the dolphins she felt certain would be waiting there for her. The note she had left two days ago said she did not know how long she would be gone. Right then, Jude decided that she would not return until she had seen dolphins. In the meantime, the cool water beckoned and she allowed it to seduce her into its wetness.

As she waited, Jude wandered the shore looking for shells, played with the hermit crabs and starfish in the tide pools, played tag with the ocean waves and swam. She loved lying flat on her belly in the water, holding her breath for as long as she could as she watched the blue, blue of the ocean. The blue went on forever, changing from a sparkling pale at the surface and deepening to a dark turquoise. Rays of the sun filtered through the blue and disappeared. Little motes of ocean plant matter and the many fishes captured the rays and reflected them back. It was spellbinding, this blue, blue ocean world.

She ate fresh mangos and the dried meat she had brought with her, drank from a nearby spring, slept under the stars with the sound of a gentle surf lulling her toward her dreams.

On the third day, they came—two of them— whispering through the water.

Jude happened to be swimming and they swirled around her, chirping and clicking in their own special language as she treaded water looking this way and that. Then, they darted off, diving deep, turning in an instant to leap high into the air, their glistening bodies spiraling toward the sun. They dove into the blue and then swirled round and round her, clicking, spiraling up and out and back in again. Jude grinned and laughed out loud.

Then one of the dolphins came up to her, so close that her fingertips just grazed its sleek side. It rolled slightly so that it could easily stare into her eyes. Looking into the eye of the dolphin was like looking into the ocean. It went on and on, that clear gaze, sparkling with humor and ancient wisdoms, a bright intelligence.

And then they were gone, as quickly as they had come, leaving behind images of spirals, sparkles and diamond water droplets.

That night, she dreamed of spirals, and in the morning as the sun burned through a blanket of fog, Jude thought of home. Perhaps it was the dolphins or perhaps it was just being away and breaking her routine, but it occurred to Jude that maybe life wasn't supposed to be a wheel of repetition. Maybe life was a spiral where the same day-to-day things occurred, but with each new moment, there was a new way to look at the sameness. Maybe the sameness was like the ocean, going on and on. Maybe if you swam through the sameness like a dolphin, occasionally leaping and spiraling out of it, then the sameness—like the ocean—was something you lived and played in. Maybe, thought Jude, just maybe it wasn't about recognition or whether your ideas were acknowledged. *Maybe* it was about playing and enjoyment. *Maybe* it was about being happy.

Jude thought about that as she rolled up her sleeping bag and cleaned up her camp. She shouldered her pack and looked at the cove, at the blue. For several moments she stood and watched the waves and the seabirds. The water was calm. Jude took a deep breath, slowly exhaled and then smiled. Turning, she began the steep ascent that would eventually lead her home.

Chapter 6
...The Magician

"Who are you going to be this time?" the boy asked.

Jude cocked an eyebrow and glanced at his direction. "That all depends on what they want," he answered with a slight smile.

The boy was about to say more, but Jude put a finger up to silence him and then turned his attention to the passing countryside outside the train's window. The movement lulled him into a mindset of meditation, and he let his thoughts roam as they pleased.

All across the continent in every place that he had stopped, he had been someone new. He had been a count, a chef, an actor, a priest, a student, a teacher, an architect, a designer, a laborer, a farmer, a juggler, and a musician. He had fed people, entertained them, taught them, and wooed them. He learned from them, buried them, married them, danced with them, designed for them, and built for them. And, above all, he had tricked them, each and every one.

Jude glanced at his fellow traveler who pretended he wasn't watching. That is, he had tricked each and every one of them *except* for the bright-eyed beggar boy.

Jude stretched and yawned lazily. "You know, Boy," he began thoughtfully, "I believe I grow weary of this game." He reached into his robes and withdrew a white dove. It left its mark where it had been, flapping its wings, downy feathers flying. The boy opened the train's window and the bird flew out as Jude dabbed at the excrement. The boy sat back and folded his arms, watching Jude who glanced up with a twinkle in his eye. "I believe I shall go as myself," he said. "And you can be my young apprentice. And, " he paused as the train began to slow, "I believe this is where we will be getting off."

Jude strode into the Grand Hotel, the boy following close at hand, lugging two large valises. With a flourish, he tapped the bell at the front desk, leaned against the counter and looked around at the charming couples parading back and forth, following the agendas they had planned for themselves.

"Yes?" The concierge inquired. "May I help you?"

"I am Carlo, The Magician," replied Jude, his gloved hand sweeping in an arch, forcing the gentleman to step back. "I would like a suite of rooms for myself and my young apprentice, here. Preferably," he added as he flicked an imaginary piece of lint from his robes, "a suite facing the back with a view of your gardens."

The boy put down the valises and wiped his nose with the back of his hand.

The concierge frowned. "And how will you pay for these rooms, sir? We require payment up front."

"Piffle!" Jude exclaimed loudly, causing heads to turn. "Carlo, The Magician *never* pays for his rooms in advance. But," he paused, raising a finger. "If you were to insist, I would give you one of *these* as payment." He reached into his robes and withdrew three gold coins. The boy's eyes widened as well as concierge's. "You see," Jude explained. "Carlo is good for the payment." And he put the coins back into his robes.

The concierge picked up a pen, dipped it in ink and authorized his approval with his signature. He then turned the guest book toward Jude and handed him the pen. As Jude signed "Carlo, The Magician" with large, looping letters, the concierge summoned a bellhop. "Please show these two guests to Suite Five at the back, " he told the bellhop, handing him a key, and smiling at Jude.

Jude bowed deeply to the concierge, and turned toward the groups of guests who were coming and going. "Good people," he stated loudly. "I am Carlo, The Magician. I bid you a 'good day' and I invite you to my magic show tonight. It begins promptly at 8:00. I give you my word. You won't be disappointed." He reached into his robes and with a courtly bow, withdrew a perfect rose, its petals glistening with dew, which he handed to a nearby woman who gasped in pleasure. "And for the Gentleman," Jude reached into his robes again, "A fine cigar," handing it to the woman's companion. The small crowd that had gathered clapped politely and with appreciation.

Jude bowed to them all. "Thank you, my charming new friends. I look forward to entertaining you this evening. I will be here for a week. And after that..." he paused,

64

grinning wickedly, "...after that you will either be the envy of those around you because you saw the Great Magician Carlo, or, you will *envy* those around you. You, of course, are free to choose."

Readjusting his robes, Jude nodded to the boy and they followed the bellhop who was waiting with their valises.

In the rooms as the boy looked out over the hotel's gardens, Jude gave instructions to the bellhop to rent a venue hall for the week. He handed him two gold coins, and the bellhop grinned when he was told he could keep the change.

That night, Jude dazzled the small crowd in attendance. The next night, the crowd was larger, and the night after that, larger still.

By week's end, it was rumored that the show would to be standing room only. The proprietor of the venue hall was delighted, as was the hotel's concierge. As word had spread, people were coming from out of town to see the Great Carlo, The Magician. No one wanted to be left out.

Combing his thick hair, Jude noticed the boy watching him in the mirror. "Yes?" he asked.

"This is the last night," said the boy.

"Ah, how right you are," Jude agreed.

"What happens now?" the boy asked.

Jude put the comb down and turned toward the boy. "Tonight?" The boy nodded. "Tonight!" Jude stated dramatically. "Why, tonight they will be eating from our hands! Tonight will be the most spectacular of all!"

"What happens?" the boy repeated.

Jude beamed at the boy. "Do you know how I bring things out of my robe? " The boy nodded. "Amazing things?" The boy nodded. "From swords to jewels..." he paused, chuckling. "Do you remember the pig?" The boy smiled. "Well," Jude said, "I shall do those things, and much more." He paused. "But, I am also going to do something they will talk about for years to come." The boy waited expectantly. "Tonight. I shall place *myself* into this very robe and," he again paused for effect. "And, my fine young lad, I shall disappear." Jude clapped his hands. "And that, will be that." Jude grinned hugely, waiting for a response from the boy. His smile faded as one, single tear trailed down the boy's solemn face.

66

"O no. No, no, no," Jude said. "We'll have none of that!" he added softly. Jude reached into his robe and withdrew a large, lacy handkerchief. Dropping down on one knee before the boy, he gently dabbed at the boy's tear. "Hush now, Boy. It's all right."

"But you will be gone," the boy whispered. "I will never see you again."

"Piffle." Jude replied. "Of *course* you will see me again. But it won't be for many, many years to come. " He raised one finger and tapped the boy on the nose. "And, mind you, you will have to look for me. For an intelligent boy like you, I won't make it easy."

The boy tried to smile and Jude hugged him. "That's my boy." He said, holding him out at arm's length. "Now, then.... Three things is all you will ever need to remember: First, is to imagine. Second, is to assume. Third, is to enjoy." He held the boy's gaze. "Understood?" The boy nodded. Jude smiled. "Such an intelligent boy!" he said affectionately.

Jude rose and adjusted his robes. "And now, the crowd is waiting to be entertained."

For many years after, people told the story of that night, the last night that The Great Carlo ever performed.

As promised, the show was spectacular. Carlo was at his apex. He dazzled. He delighted. And then, at the end, he took off his robes and held them out, turning them this way and that way so that the crowd could see that the robes were empty.

Next, he turned toward his apprentice and held up one finger, a second finger and then a third.

Carlo the Magician waited for the boy to nod and then drew a figure eight in the air.

With that, he flung the robes high over his head in one final, grand gesture. The robes swirled above him, then around him, and then settled themselves softly upon the stage floor. Carlo, The Magician was no longer there. Carlo, The Magician had vanished.

The stunned crowd was silent.

In the silence, the young apprentice stooped down and picked up the robes. He quietly arranged them about his shoulders.

The boy had either grown or the robes had shortened, but they fit him perfectly.

Chapter 7 ...Death

Jude gazed lovingly at her beloved. "When you were in the hospital..." she said, "...on life support, and it was just you and me... and the machines...I felt like I was covered in this huge soft peach blanket. It was delicious. I felt safe and loved and, even though this was supposed to be the most tragic of all events, I felt...okay.... like it was all perfect, just as it should be.

"Then when you came back, I looked into your eyes, those feelings came back, too, but they were...." She shrugged..."I don't know...it was like the genie got put back into the bottle or something...like we're all genies and our bodies are the bottles."

He looked at her and smiled. "I don't

remember any of it," he said. "My first memory is pulling those god-awful tubes out of my nose and calling the nurse who insisted upon shoving them back in *a black hearted bitch*."

Jude smiled and stroked his arm. "That had to have hurt! And, I remember you felt badly calling her those things, too."

Her expression grew thoughtful. "I wonder what this is all about...this life and death stuff. You didn't ever feel 'dead' to me. You felt expanded or something."

He grinned. "Like a genie out of the bottle."

"Exactly." She smiled. "And I got my wish, too, because you came back to me. I really didn't want to live the rest of my life without you."

"I don't understand why people get so upset about death," he said. "Death is as natural as birth. Yet, when I think of people I love dying, it makes me sad. It makes me want to stop this conversation," he sat up and swung his legs over the side of the bed, "and get up and take a shower and get on with my day."

Jude laughed as he did exactly that. She sat up, reached for her robe and headed for the kitchen and coffee. But her mind wouldn't

72

allow her to leave the subject of life and death. And she gazed out the window, cup of coffee in hand, deep in thought.

She knew that life and death was a natural cycle, and that lots of things died...not just the physical bodies. Ideas died. Theories died. Businesses died. When one thought about those things, they were saddened for a while if attached to them. Then, if you embraced what was new, it wasn't that bad. Death and life. Life and death. Death and life. Cycle and recycle.

That didn't feel right to her. There had to be more to it. Her eye caught the plant on the window sill. It was in full bloom. Yet, there were new blooms, mature blooms and dying blooms, all on the same plant, all at the same time. The dying blooms had fulfilled their purpose and were letting go. The nutrients that fed the blooms were withdrawing back into the plant so that they could go into one of the growing buds. Birth and re-birth, birth and re-birth...all on the same plant...all at the same time.

Jude took a sip of her coffee, still studying the plant. So, if the plant was continually living and dying, what then, exactly was life? What was the constant?? The movement of a hummingbird caught her eye. She watched as a tiny feather came loose and floated from its body. Things were constantly living and dying on the hummingbird as well. What was the constant there...the living and dying? Or was there something more?

Jude turned from the window and leaned against the countertop, coffee-in-hand, staring at nothing. She imagined she was high up in space, looking at the beautiful, blue earth spinning in the black. On the earth, there was constant life and death. Her thoughts wandered back to the hospital room when she had felt her beloved all around her as the "genie out of the bottle."

Suddenly it all clicked.

The constant was the life force. It was the divinity, that creative consciousness, of each living/dying cycle—connecting everything to each other and to all things. So, whether or not the genie was in or out of the bottle, it was still a genie.

People grieve for the loss of loved ones because they are looking at the bottle and not the genie. So how, Jude supposed, does one learn not to grieve when faced with death? Because when presented with the possibility of her beloved's death, it was his closeness that she grieved. His voice, his touch. The way he looked at her. She wanted the genie back in the bottle!

It was a learning process, she realized. Because when her beloved genie was "out of the bottle" she still felt him. She knew it! He had been all around her, so close to her and so loving. It was the emotional response that she had toward that experience that made her know, deep within her, that he was with her. It was only when she mourned him, that she felt the separation. The mourning disconnected her from his huge, loving presence because her sorrow veiled the fact he was still the genie, only out of the bottle. It was that simple. When she loved him, she connected with him. When she missed him and longed for him, she was disconnected.

Perhaps people wouldn't grieve so much when loved ones died—whether it be other people, pets or even projects, if they focused more on the genies than on their bottles while they were still in their bottles. What if she looked for the divinity in all the things that crossed her path that day? What if she practiced a new way of connecting with her pets and her loved ones? What if she could recognize their love and connection to her, not depending on if they were in or out of their genie bottles?

Jude smiled. There was so much more to learn, but she felt much freer from the grieving process. She knew she was on the right track, and that felt very good indeed.

Chapter 8 ...The Lovers

They sat holding hands, foreheads and knees together, their bodies forming a heart. And they giggled like children with secrets.

Jude smiled at the photograph on the gallery wall. The subjects weren't children. They were her grandparents, well into their eighties. She sighed, so much love there, and moved to the next.

In this piece, there were three photos matted in one frame of a young man and his fiancée. By his stance, one could tell that he was shy and insecure. From his expression, you could tell he was very much in love and couldn't believe his good luck. The young woman was stunning. She held herself with the confidence of one who always had gotten what she wanted. In the first photograph, the pair seemed to be totally mismatched. The beautiful young woman was slightly in front of the man. Her eyes looked flint-like and hard. In the second, the two were looking at each other—he with adoration, she looking slightly bemused but tolerant. The third photograph told a different story. Jude had taken it right after the photo session was over, when the two were completely unaware. The beautiful young woman's head was tilted sideways, her cheek resting on the young man's hand that she had positioned there herself. Looking into his eyes, she smiled and it was that smile that Jude wanted to capture in the photograph, and had. It was a smile that two lovers share in private when they both took off their masks they created for themselves. It was that smile of joy when someone finds another with total acceptance.

Jude was proud of the images she had captured in the trio of photographs. She moved on.

The show was entitled *Lovers*. The feeling Jude wanted the viewers to take home was one of hope, that love between couples did not have to be fleeting. Fairy tale endings can happen. Although many of the couples in the photographs did not look as if they had lived "happily ever after," it was evident they had been through hardships together. In all the photographs of the older couples, there was a strength and peace emanating from the images resulting from the years together. By knowing that there was someone in their lives they could count on, they were undeniably dependent upon one another.

As she scanned the room looking at all the photographs, Jude felt certain she had accomplished her goal. The love from the couples was palpable.

Jude had shot hundreds of photographs of all different couples, all different genders, ages, nationalities, and traditions. She tried to capture representations of all different kinds of love between two people she could think of. Her only criteria was that the viewer could not doubt the shared love depicted in the images was real, strong, and permanent.

Her hard work had paid off.

The exception was the photograph before her. She had no idea why she had decided to display it with the others. It allowed doubt into the room. In Jude's hand was another framed photograph she had brought with her to exchange. But she paused, contemplating the image.

81

It was a black and white self-portrait, backlit, soft, shot in the style of a 1940s Hollywood glamour shot. She had draped herself in a white gauzy fabric and she was sitting on a stool in her studio with another stool beside her on which was placed a fluted glass of champagne. Her eyes were demurely cast down and she was bare-breasted, however an observer wouldn't really pay attention to that.

What they would notice and take home in their memories was the angry, puckered, barely healed scars that slashed across her chest and breasts. "Would the memory of this image cast out the memories of all the portraits of love that surrounded this photograph?" Jude, the artist contemplated.

She had kept the self-portrait for two reasons. One was because she wanted that question answered. The other was if it were not for the brutality she had experienced, she would never have been able to show the world what the permanence of true love looked like.

Jude reached out in hesitation. Hearing her name called by the gallery owner, she quickly made a decision and turned to prepare her state of mind for the reception.
The next day, the critics' reviews were glowing with admiration for Jude's show and

work. Her private and business lines had not stopped ringing with congratulatory calls.

Not one critic, not one caller mentioned her self-portrait.

Jude was satisfied.

Chapter 9

...The Chariot

"You are at the top of your game, sir," Jude's Captain of the Guard said as he reached for the sword that Jude had just twisted out of his hands.

Jude laughed. He could still feel the adrenaline flowing through his body. He felt immortal. "I am inclined to agree with you, my friend," he replied. "But, that would be foolish wouldn't it?" He returned the sword to the man. "Thank you for the exercise. As always, I have learned something new."

The Captain of the Guard bowed.

Jude made his way to his private gardens where he liked to go to think and to problem solve. It was a large garden and looked more like a natural setting, rather than a planned landscape; its paths meandering along a hillside.

"At the top of my game," Jude thought. "Am I, indeed, at the top of my game?"

Running a hand through his thick, long hair, he looked back at his life. He hadn't always been where he stood today. True, he was born of privilege, but he wasn't treated that way. His mother died at childbirth and his father had sent him away to be nurtured and raised by a poor relative whose wealth consisted of kindness. In that setting, he was one of many. He worked and fought and played right along side his childhood friends, never the wiser he was heir to anything, let alone his own kingdom.

In his nineteenth year, his father reclaimed him and Jude's life became one of military tactics, governing and study. His father was a good king, a fair king and well respected. He was generous with his knowledge and Jude was wise enough to listen and learn. When his father turned the kingdom over to Jude, he was ready.

Now, it was eight years later. His father had remained as Jude's advisor until his death two years ago. Fortunate enough to marry for love, Jude and his Queen were expecting their first child. Here he stood, in his thirty-ninth year, supposedly at the top of his game, pondering what happened next.

Rounding a corner, he heard a quiet humming and he smiled, recognizing its source.

The Queen, his beloved, sat alone on an ornate swing overlooking a small pond. Glancing up, she smiled and reached out her hand toward him. Jude returned her smile, allowing her hand to guide him to sit beside her.

"I am at the top of my game," he told her, after a few moments of quiet companionship.

She cocked her head at him, raising an eyebrow. "Indeed?"

He nodded. "So I've been told."

"Ah," she replied. "What is it like?"

"What is it like?" Jude repeated and then, with a laugh replied, "That's for the chronicles to describe. I have no time as I'm living it."

Jude put a hand on her rounded belly, feeling the life within. "And how is our son?"

"Our son is fine," replied the Queen. "I do not

know who is more ready for this birth," she continued, "him or me. However, we'll need to wait another few months."

Jude smiled and leaned in for a kiss, "As will I."

They sat in comfortable silence before Jude spoke again. "There is a king on my northern border who would like to extend his property. I thought I would pay him a visit. Care to come along?"

His Queen smiled. "I would hate to miss a man at the top of his game enter into negotiations with a greedy king."

Lion and his brother pulled the chariot across the great northern plain that ran the border of Jude's kingdom. Jude mused, as he watched Lion's muscles work under his tawny hide. When he was a young cub, Jude had asked Lion how he wanted to be named. Lion thought it was an odd question as "Lion" said everything about him that he was. Now as Jude watched, he realized Lion was right. It was the perfect name.

"I see them," said the Queen, pointing.

Jude looked in the direction of the Queen's finger. "Ah, so you do. He looks like he means business, does he not?"

The army camped on his borders was vast, but Jude focused his gaze on the large tent with the fluttering banners and directed Lion to that destination. As they neared, the crowd parted to let him pass, gazing in wonder at the sight of two great beasts pulling a chariot. As the chariot slowed to a stop in front of the tent, Lion roared, forcing the crowd of warriors back. When the tent flap parted and the raiding king—a few years younger than Jude—came into view, Lion growled. Lion looked back and yawned a great cat yawn, showing all his teeth, causing Jude to chuckle.

Jude jumped down with a smile. "A good morning to you!" He said. "I am called Jude, the king of this land, and this is my Queen. I thought I'd come and see why you wish to invade my kingdom."

The invading king looked at Jude as if he were insane. He glanced at the lions and then at the Queen who smiled at him with the secret contented smile of a woman with child. He glanced back at the lions. "The lions," he said, "they have no reins."

"That is very true," Jude replied. "Shall we go inside to discuss these things? My lovely Queen, as you can see, is in a delicate condition and the chariot ride has tired her."

The raiding king nodded, still glancing at the lions as Jude helped his Queen down from the chariot. Shaking his head as if trying to remember something, the reluctant host gestured to one of his generals. "Bring something to drink for my...er....guests."

"And some water for my lions." Jude added. "They've come a long way."

As he and the queen ducked into the tent, Jude said to the two guards posted at the entrance, "Don't be alarmed, they will only bite at my bidding."

It was cool inside the tent. The water was refreshing and tasted of mint. The Queen sighed with pleasure, causing the visiting leader to glance in her direction. She smiled at him with a smile of a woman who knew her value and knew she was loved.

"I am sure," Jude began, "that you think I am a fool to arrive in the midst of your great army with my Queen without even one warrior as escort."

90

The other king nodded slowly, unsure what Jude's "game" was.

Jude's gaze and tone hardened. "I can assure you sir, I am no fool."

He snorted. "Not a fool? You and your Queen are surrounded by my army! Who is to stop me from either capturing or killing you?"

"I do not feel that is an issue," Jude replied. "It would be virtually impossible for you to give orders with your throat torn out." Both lions roared from directly outside the tent. "My lions might die, but they would kill you first."

The king visibly paled. "Then why are you here?"

"I told you," Jude replied. "I am curious as to why you wish to extend your borders to include my kingdom."

The king stared at Jude. "I do believe you *are* mad," he said. "Your kingdom is a fertile and abundant nation. I want it to improve my own holdings. I have the power to take it, and I shall."

"Because we are peaceable does not mean we cannot protect ourselves," Jude answered. "I am not the only one who drives a chariot pulled by two lions without reins."

He waved his hand as if swatting at a fly. "But that is a moot point. I am very curious as to why a king would want to gather an army of men to march clear across his kingdom and arrive, tired and weakened at the borders of a neighboring kingdom to attack it." He paused, leaning forward, "...when he can create his own fertile and abundant kingdom using the muscle power of his army without incurring loss of life?"

The other king laughed. "Why would I want to *build* a kingdom, when I can take yours?"

Jude laughed in return. "*Supposing* you could take my fertile and abundant land, you do not know how to maintain it—which obviously you don't or you wouldn't want mine—then your new kingdom would rapidly begin to look like your old one."

The other king blinked. "Why do you say that?"

"Because a kingdom reflects its ruler, and were you to rule the kingdom that is now mine, it would begin to look like yours does." Jude sat back. "Now, if it were I, I would want to know how I could make my kingdom as fertile and abundant as my neighbor's before I gathered my armies and tried to conquer my neighbor. If it were I, I would learn from my neighbor.

Then, when I wanted to extend my borders, I would know I could increase the value of all of my land, as well as maintain the newly acquisitioned one."

The hopeless conqueror sat in silence, absently rubbing his bearded chin. "So you are telling me to ask for your help to make my own kingdom rich and abundant before I invade yours?"

Jude shook his head. "No, I merely told you what I would do were I ruling your kingdom. I can tell you," he added, "it is of much more economic value to make strong what you already possess. Surely you were taught that the whole kingdom is only as mighty as its hub and that you can only reinforce an empire from the inside out."

The invader became thoughtful. Then he spoke once more with a calculating gleam in his eye, "You would be willing to teach me how to make my holdings rich and abundant?"

"Absolutely," Jude replied. "I would much rather do that than wage war with you. War takes so much time out of our planting schedule. It annoys the entire kingdom. I shall send some of my most qualified farmers and stewards to accompany you back so you can get started. We are about to enter the planting season and the timing couldn't be better for you to begin to enrich your kingdom."

Jude stood as did the other king and they clasped hands, smiling. Others could handle the final negotiations now that the two kings were in agreement.

Jude turned toward his Queen, "Are you rested enough for the return journey, my dear?" he asked.

The new compatriot looked at the Queen and her husband with envy, as Jude gently pulled her to her feet.

Outside the tent, the lions were already standing.

The king turned toward his generals. "There will be no battle this year," he told them. "King Jude and I have come to an agreement that will be better for the kingdom."

The news traveled fast among the foot soldiers. There was some grumbling but mostly cheering. Many were farmers and knew the value of planting on time.

After saying good-bye and bidding a good return journey, Jude helped his queen into the chariot, then stepped in beside her.

Lion turned the chariot around and with a mighty roar, he and his brother began the long trek home.

The Queen put her hand on Jude's.

He glanced at her. "Well?" he asked.

"You know he still means to attack after his country has stabilized," she said.

Jude laughed. "It is what I would do," he answered. And laughed again. "He has no idea the effort it takes to maintain a healthy and satisfied kingdom. He will be too busy to plan an invasion for several years to come. Of that I will make certain."

The Queen cocked her head at him. "You know," she remarked, "I do believe you are at the top of your game."

Chapter 10
...The Universe

I danced under the stars and the Universe was mine.

I danced with my spirit and the Universe was mine.

I looked this way and saw the movement of the wind. I looked that way and saw stars.

And the Universe was mine.

I looked to those I needed to forgive and I forgave and the Universe was mine.

I looked to those who sought hope and I gave them hope and the Universe was mine.

I sipped the life of the colors and we shared

and the light fed us and the Universe was mine.

I unhooked from guilt and the Universe was mine.

I unhooked from fear and the Universe was mine.

I reached and my heart opened and the Universe was mine.

I stepped from the shadows into the stunning light and the Universe was mine.

I danced with the shadows and we laughed and spun together and the Universe was mine.

The Universe swallowed me up and it was mine.

I gave all that I am to the Universe and it gave me back to me.

I am the Universe and the Universe is mine.

XV

The Devil

Chapter 11 ...The Devil

The pub owner wiped down his bar in slow, steady circles. He glanced over at the corner table where the young man wrote feverously in a journal. "'Tis Sunday, Lad," he said, "Pub closes early."

Jude looked up from his journal, his eyes refocusing. It took him a moment to register that he'd been spoken to. "Oh, yeah, sure," he mumbled. He looked around, noticing the pub was empty. "Sorry," he added.

Grabbing his messenger bag at his feet, Jude stuffed his journal and pen into it. He fished around in his jeans pocket for some money to pay for his pint. Laying it on the table, he headed toward the front door. The waitress smiled at him as she let him out and locked the door in his wake.

Outside the pub, Jude paused for a moment looking up at the tall buildings surrounding him. It was a quiet time and he imagined the millions of the city's inhabitants back in their homes, comfortable and asleep. He smiled sarcastically at his romanticized point of view, knowing full well not everyone was asleep. For that matter, not everyone had homes.

Between the buildings he could see the moon, full and bright.

Adjusting his bag, Jude headed to his apartment asking himself for the umpteenth time what the hell he was doing in the city.

Jude didn't like the smell. He didn't like the noise. He didn't like the crowds. He didn't like living in a cramped, expensive apartment. He didn't like the roommates he needed just to afford the apartment. And he didn't like the job he had in order to pay for the "luxury."

The only place Jude really felt at home was the pub he had just left. Yet, here he was, walking back to his cramped and too expensive apartment filled with roommates just like he'd been doing for the past five years.

His friends from the university had all followed their dreams, he thought bitterly—

living interesting lives that he could follow on Facebook. Whereas Jude, at twenty-eight, was still working the small administrative positions in various publishing houses as he wrote reams and reams of novels that never quite lived up to his satisfaction, so were never submitted for publication.

In school, Jude had learned to "write about what you know." Taking that to heart, Jude had made it the one rule that he continuously adhered to. The problem was in his mind's eye, Jude really didn't think he knew much about anything, and he really had no idea how to make that change.

Jude had written ten novels—*ten novels*, each with a young man as protagonist, filled with angst and ennui, who found himself living in a city he hated, suffering through events that were tedious and lackluster.

Inserting his key in his apartment door, Jude opened it quietly and slipped into his room, the one closest to the front door. He undressed in the dark and lay in bed listening to the soft snores of his roommates until he fell asleep.

The next evening, Jude found himself back at his favorite table at the pub, writing furiously.

103

"What are you writing?" the waitress asked as she set down his pint of lager.

Jude barely registered that he had been spoken to. He mumbled his thanks, took a drink, and went back to writing. The waitress glanced over at her father, the proprietor behind the bar, smiled ruefully and shrugged.

The proprietor smiled and shook his head, pouring a pint for another customer.

The pub was well established and had a steady flow of customers. They usually began arriving around lunchtime and would keep the entire staff busy until closing. It was a family of sorts. Everyone knew each other. Everyone, that is, except for the lad who sat alone at table 15--Jude.

The proprietor had been keeping an eye on Lad 15, as he had affectionately called him. He'd seen several Lad 15s in his establishment, in his lifetime. This one seemed a little more downcast than others, but he continued to have hope for him. He was a handsome young man, despite the scowl and closed expression, tall and lean, had his own sense of style that the proprietor liked—a loner, and an individual.

Lad 15 first began showing up about six months ago. It had been cold, so cold that few had ventured out and the pub was relatively empty. Jude had paused just inside the front door for several moments, deciding whether or not to stay. Finally, the young man had selected a table--table 15--and had become a regular. For that entire time, the proprietor had never seen him speak with anyone, unless ordering his nightly lager.

"I've got him good, this one," came a voice from behind the pub owner.

The proprietor cocked his head toward the voice. "I've been expectin' ye," he said. "The usual?" He poured two shots of a hundred-year-old scotch into a glass and slid it over to the handsome, well-dressed man at the counter.

"Don't mind if I do," said the devil and took a sip, savoring its smoky flavor and bite.

Placing the bottle within easy reach of his guest, the proprietor said, "Help yerself, it's on the house."

"Much obliged," said the devil, taking another sip from his glass. "I plan to be here awhile."

105

"Don't doubt that," the proprietor responded, glancing at the young man at table 15. The lad's brow was furrowed with concentration. At the same time he was sipping from his own pint, the proprietor noticed the devil taking a swallow of his scotch. "So you think you've got him?" he asked.

The devil smiled with satisfaction. "What do you think?"

Before he could answer, the pub owner's daughter came up to place an order from a nearby table. She glanced nervously at the handsome man who winked at her as he calmly sipped his drink. The proprietor poured the drinks and patted her hand where it grasped the tray, letting her know the order was filled. She smiled, with troubled eyes, and left.

"I think," the proprietor replied, "that all of humankind has free will, and the freedom to exercise it whenever it wants to."

"Or not," said the devil.

"Or not," agreed the proprietor.

The devil tilted back his head and drained the glass. He slapped his hands on the counter and rose. "I've changed my mind. I believe I shall move on. Thanks for the drink and the conversation."

"Anytime," said the proprietor, taking away the used glass and recapping the bottle. By the time he finished wiping off the bar, the devil had disappeared.

He noticed that the young man at table 15 was staring off into space with a gloomy expression. Deciding it was time he went over to visit this Lad 15, he called over his daughter to tend the bar.

The proprietor delivered another pint to Jude and sat down across from him. "On the house," the bartender said, smiling, when Jude glanced up.

Surprised, Jude nodded his thanks and took a sip.

"So," the proprietor began, "You've been comin' here for a fair few weeks now, lad. Thought I'd say hello. You a writer?"

Jude nodded wryly. "Attempting to be. I've written ten books so far."

The proprietor raised his eyebrows. "Ten?

That's quite a lot. You're a published author, then? That's quite good."

Jude snorted. "I wish! They're," he paused, searching for words, "they're too bloody boring!" he exclaimed. "I've never submitted any. Who'd want to read them?"

"Boring? How so."

Jude shrugged and sat back, folding his arms. "You know how they say to write about what you know?"

The proprietor nodded.

"Well," said Jude, "I do, but my life is so, I don't know, the same, that my books are all the same. I start them out differently, but they always end up being about a guy in a city where nothing really exciting happens to him." Jude paused. "This is going to be my last book. Then I think I'm going to give up."

"And do what?"

Jude shrugged. "I dunno. Go home I suppose. Continue to live my dead end life in the dead end town where I grew up. Build and repair stonewalls like my father does, like my grandfather did before him and like my great-

108

grandfather did before them both," he added bitterly.

The proprietor smiled. "Aren't you a little young to be giving up?"

"I'm twenty-eight. In two years I'll be thirty with nothing to show for myself." He opened his hands wide. "For crisssakes, all my flatmates are barely in their twenties! They get good jobs and they move out, new, younger ones, take their place, and so on." Jude took a drink and wiped his mouth on his sleeve. "I'm so stuck."

The proprietor nodded in understanding. "I hear ye, Lad. Many a young fella feel like you do...and, y'know? Yer not really stuck."

Jude stared at the older man for a few moments, then sighed, running his hand through his thick, unruly hair. "Look, Sir, I appreciate you trying to make me feel better. But, I *am* stuck. I think I know my life a little better than you since I'm living it."

"Aye, most likely," the self-proclaimed sage replied mildly. "So, let's talk about your writing then."

Jude snorted. "It's stuck, too."

"Writer's Block?"

"More like 'This-Writer's-Life-Block.' I write what I know and I don't know much." Jude laughed. "So, I write more of *that!*"

"Well, that's where imagination comes in to play," the proprietor said. "Do you think Tolkien ever lived with Hobbits? Or Jules Verne ever take a journey in a submarine?" He glanced over at the bar and saw his daughter scowling at him. "Och, I need to go, lad." He cocked his head at the girl, "My daughter's lookin' a tad peeved."

Jude followed his gaze and, for the first time, noticed the waitress who had been serving him these many weeks. "Is she your daughter?" he asked the bartender. "She's...," he paused.

"She is lovely, isn't she?" agreed the proprietor. "And she doesn't put up with much nonsense, so I best be goin' now." He stood and squeezed Jude's shoulder. "Perhaps you should write what your imagination knows, rather than what you know. Perhaps write what you would like to happen, rather than what is happening. Only a suggestion, mind." He winked at Jude and traded places with his daughter.

110

Several weeks later the proprietor heard that familiar voice requesting a large dram from a 100-year-old-bottle of scotch.

He turned, smiled at his distinguished guest as he reached for the bottle and began to pour. He set the drink and the bottle down in front of his customer saying, "Help yerself. It's on the house."

The devil reached for the glass, took a drink, savoring the flavor. "Not this time," he replied. "I believe I'll pay for this drink."

The proprietor raised an eyebrow.

"How'd you do it?" the devil asked.

The proprietor glanced over at the lad at table 15 who was in a deep conversation with his daughter. He smiled. "I just reminded him of a few things."

The devil sighed, taking another drink. After a few moments, he spoke, "Well, he's got free will. He can forget, I suppose."

The proprietor chuckled. "I doubt it. He's in love."

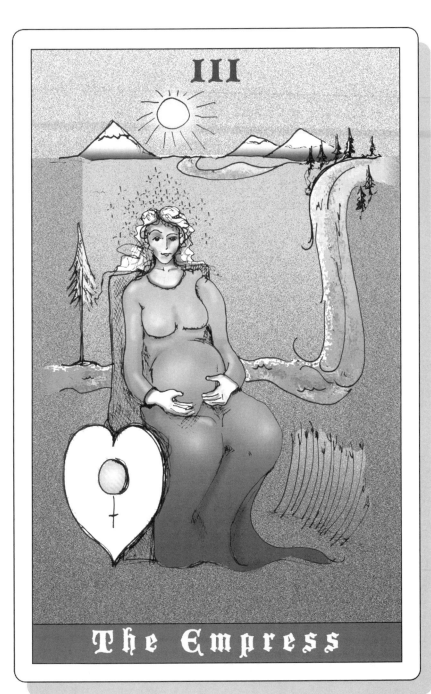

Chapter 12
...The Empress

The rain was falling in sheets, creating mud and ruts in the road. In the pre-dawn hours Jude stumbled. It wasn't the first time she had slipped and nearly fallen into the ditch along the well-travelled road. Regaining her balance, she sighed and shifted her pack, wondering if she had made the right decision.

It had seemed like a good idea the night before when there wasn't a cloud in the sky and the balmy air smelled of apple and peach blossoms. Impatient and wanting to move on, she had packed her belongings, checked out of her room and walked a few miles down the road toward the next town. A blossoming apple tree, alone in a meadow dotted with spring flowers, had offered shelter. She had drifted off to sleep in comfort, awaking to a downpour and rivulets of water streaming into her bedroll.

Fortunately her pack, hanging on one of the apple tree branches, had remained dry, so Jude began her rainy journey in relative comfort. But now, only the contents of her oil skinned canvas pack remained dry. And Jude was beginning to worry about her health, which she wanted to hold on to. She was freezing cold and her teeth were beginning to sound like castanets.

Sighing, Jude stopped. The rain ran off her body in mini-torrents, running into her boots. "Okay, you win," she said calmly. "Help me, please," she added, rather proud that she managed to be polite.

Within minutes, a handsome and sturdy coach drawn by two silver grey horses rolled to a stop beside her. The door opened and the smell and warmth of mid-summer beckoned her. An outstretched hand grasped hers pulling Jude into the dry comfort. Jude's mother smiled at her and handed her a large, fluffy pale pink towel.

Jude took the towel and mopped her face and hair before slipping her pack from her shoulders and placing it on the floor under the coach's seat. Her mother smiled and handed her a large robe that matched the towel.

Jude stripped the wet clothing from her body. It clung in places, splattering water as she wrestled it from her body. She let it fall in a mound at her feet. Quickly donning the robe, feeling their absorbent fibers drying her, Jude allowed the warmth to relax her.

She settled into the carriage seat across from her mother, slipping her feet into the pink slippers that awaited her and sighed with pure pleasure and comfort. For the first time that entire night, she smiled. The carriage rocked gently as the powerful horses pulled it through the rain.

Looking into her mother's green eyes, Jude smiled and said, "Thank you."

Jude's mother looked into her daughter's green eyes and smiled. "You are quite welcome."

Jude closed her eyes, briefly leaning her head back against the dark red leather headrest. "Tea?" she proposed, opening her eyes.

Her mother handed her a cup and saucer filled with a blend of rose hips and chamomile. She deeply inhaled before taking a sip, enjoying how the warmth of the tea spread throughout her body.

"That was rather unpleasant, Mother," she said.

Her mother feigned innocence. "The tea, darling? But it's your favorite."

Jude snorted. "You know what I mean. The rain."

"Ah," her mother replied.

Jude looked at her mother sitting across from her. She was wearing a rich green gown that balanced beautifully her deep auburn hair, which cascaded about her. Her green eyes glowed and sparkled with life, good will and love for her daughter.

Jude returned her mother's smile before taking the time to observe and appreciate her surroundings. The little lanterns swinging on their hangers cast lacy patterns that danced across the interior. The rich, red tooled-leather made her feel warm and safe, but she realized it was really her mother who made her feel warm and safe.

"Mother, if you continue rescuing me, how am I ever going to gain the experience to assume your position?"

116

"But you have already," her mother calmly answered her. "All you need ever know is to ask and allow. And, when it is your time to take my place, all you ever need to know is to listen and give."

"You know it is not that simple, Mother," Jude scoffed.

"And *you* know that thinking that way is why it seems so complicated."

Changing the subject, Jude frowned and proclaimed, "I was doing just fine until you made it rain. I did not ask for rain."

"No, but you did want to get to your next destination in a hurry, did you not?" Jude nodded. "Besides, I missed you and wanted to see you. I thought this a perfect solution for us both."

Jude grinned. "Just like you, Mother."

They sat in comfortable silence. Jude glanced out the window of the rocking carriage, sipping her tea and enjoying the first light of dawn. "It's stopped. The rain," she reported.

"Of course it has, dear," replied her mother. "It looks like it will be a lovely spring day."

117

Jude nodded and continued deep in thought.

"What have you been learning?" her mother asked.

Jude glanced at her mother. "That I love life. I love everything about it."

Her mother nodded. "Are you ever coming home again?"

Jude smiled. "Trick question, Mother. I am home wherever I am."

Her mother chuckled, a deep throaty laugh, which promised abundance.

The carriage slowed to a stop. "Looks like we're here," Jude said. She glanced down to where her once-soaked pile of clothes lay neatly dried and folded. "I could have done that," she said, adding, "...but thank you, Mother."

"Oh, thank you for allowing me to adventure with you," her mother replied.

Jude redressed and picked up her pack. She slung it over one shoulder, careful of her surroundings and the hanging lanterns.

118

"What are you being?" her mother asked.

"A wandering minstrel and juggler," Jude replied. "It's been fun."

"No mandolin?"

"When I need one," Jude replied before melting into her embrace. "I can't wait to see you again!"

"I can't wait to hear more."

Jude jumped out of the carriage and into the dawn. Hesitating with one hand on the carriage door, she said "I learned one other thing. I learned that you just need to ask once."

Chapter 13 ...The Tower

The night was very still, and very cold. Jude could see his breath along with the breath of the others down the line as he lay flat on his belly, waiting. The waiting was hard enough, but not as hard as what was next. Someone quietly coughed, sounding loud to his ears. He could feel the whole unit tense as if it were one great animal, then gradually relaxed back into the stillness, alert and ready.

The tower had to come down. Jude knew that now. But before he accepted this mission, he had to be convinced of that. His superiors had shown him facts and charts and graphs that all lead to that one conclusion: unless the tower came down, there would be no change. It was the tower or it was surrender.

Jude had been convinced, hand-picking his men out of the group of volunteers. These men were the best of his battalion. There wasn't much likelihood of survival and he wanted his people to know that at the get-go, so he told them and still they had volunteered. He was proud to have them by his side, to be one of them.

Now here they all were, waiting for the signal.

The tower rose from a cliff face with only three sides to defend. The plan was to flank it on all three sides, starting the attack simultaneously from all three lines. The power had already been cut a few days earlier. Jude thought they should have waited longer, but his superiors wanted the campaign to look like a seige, rather than what they were actually planning—attack and destroy. Knock the tower to the ground and everyone with it. Spare none.

In extreme peril, it had been discovered that there was a secret way into the tower—an ancient tunnel carved out of the rock walls of the cliff face. That was where Jude and his men were stationed—loaded up with explosives like pack mules. Their mission was to take out the lookouts, the snipers, and the guards. Then, rush into the tunnel and

122

plant the explosives deep at the heart of the tower, its base, and all supporting walls, set the timers, and get out. It was a plausible plan because of the simultaneous attack on the three other sides, but it was suicide as well. When he had told his men, one of them piped up, saying that the only certainty was that they'd get a medal on their caskets, but a medal was a medal. Everyone had laughed.

The night the power had been cut, Jude and five others had positioned themselves around the mouth of the tunnel so they would be able to observe exactly how it would be protected without the benefit of the bright search lights from the parapets above. Fortunately, for a secret entrance to remain a secret, it really couldn't be protected with anything that would attract attention. The enemy had dug mines and had made other deadly traps in the surrounding rocky area, leaving only a small path of safety. A path that Jude and his men now knew.

A single flare shot into the still, cold air, a faint pop announcing itself right before it burst into a red glow that reflected off the cliffs and the walls of the tower. From where they stood, Jude could hear the shouts and the rapid cracks of machine guns and mortars as the attack commenced. The familiar sound of war.

The plan was for Jude's unit to wait ten minutes for the battle to be well underway before they would commence, figuring they had another ten minutes to get the job completely done and get out. Jude, along with his five scouts, rose and carefully walked along the line of men toward the head of the unit. Out of the corner of his eye, he could see the men privately preparing in the last ten minutes of calm. Some were checking their ammo, some adjusting the explosives on their packs; he even saw one man saying a quiet prayer. Another he watched looking at a battered photo that he kissed and put back into a breast pocket. Others kissed a St. Michael's charm, a cross, and a Star of David. A few had their hands out for Jude to grasp as he passed. "Been good serving with you, sir," one man whispered. Jude nodded.

Jude and the five were the only men unburdened by explosives. They called themselves "the Linebackers" for the thirty quarterbacks carrying death on their backs. They needed to be quick. As they neared the front of the line, they began their own private preparations. Quickening their pace, and, as if with one mind, they started a quiet jog that the men behind them silently mimicked. Their luck held at the beginning. Jude and the five knew exactly where the snipers were, catching a few by surprise before the alarm went out. When it did, all hell broke.

If you could get them to talk, most would agree that the most frightening sound in battle was the sound of the bullets whipping by so close you could feel the breeze of their passing. On this night, the bullets flew thick. One opening was a very hard place to attack and easy to defend—especially if that opening was the mouth of a hornets' nest.

Three of the scouts went down. Jude couldn't tell if they were merely wounded. He could only hope for the best for them and move forward. Their luck held, and Jude and the remaining two snipers made it to the tunnel's mouth. As best they could, they formed a ring of protection for the "Mules," the thirty men carrying explosives. In training, the men had started calling themselves "Pack Mules," and then "Mules." It was a joke that morphed into a title of pride.

"Mules!" shouted Jude. The thirty men began their dash, guns firing, crossing the opening that Jude and his men made for them. One man was hit instantly, exploding into pieces. But fear didn't exist on that battlefield. The rest of the Mules became even more determined to reach their goal. There were thirty men, but only five had to make it into tower to take it out. The odds were with them, Jude thought, even if luck was running out.

As the men began coming across the clearing, Jude drew his knife, preparing to go into the tunnel's opening. He knew it was going to be close and chaotic. Their enemy couldn't risk gunfire until the tunnel widened, and neither could the attackers. He signaled to the two remaining snipers forming a wedge behind him. The last two Mules would close and barricade the doorway to the tunnel as planned.

It was about that time that Jude's mind turned into what he called "battle thinking." He became two people—the man-in-the-action and the observer-calling-the-shots. It was a paradox that puzzled him, but he'd learned early on to not question it and to use the advantages it offered. He'd never talked about it, so he never knew if others experienced "battle thinking." But he assumed that every soldier who survived over and over had something similar going on in their head. How else can anyone go through that horror time and again and come out sane?

"Captain! Sir!" one of the scouts called. He

126

was a short distance down the corridor from Jude. They had been so focused on killing and staying alive that Jude was now surprised how far into the tower they had penetrated. His scout stood at a spot where many corridors converged. From those tunnels came the cries and sounds of countless booted feet. With all the echoes it was hard to tell where they had come from.

Then Jude caught sight of the person his scout had gripped by the arm and his eyes widened. A woman! What was a woman, an obviously unarmed woman, doing alone, deep within this mayhem? She wasn't by herself, he noticed. A man stood by her, equally unarmed, equally pale and small, wearing filthy clothing. *Who were these people?* "Sir...?" the scout began.

"Quickly!" interrupted the woman. "This way...quickly...bring everyone you can this way..." She looked insistently into Jude's eyes. "Or die."

Jude's inner-observer over-ruled his inner-man-of-action. "Bring the Mules!" he shouted to the two remaining sharpshooters. They instantly followed his command.

Jude took off after the couple, who were faster

than their slight forms characterized, instinctively knowing his men were close behind.

Through endless twists and turns, Jude and his men followed the man and woman. The only sounds were the clink of buckles, and tramping feet and labored breathing. Far in the distance came a burst of gunfire and silence followed by an explosion that trembled the very foundations of the tower. With a sinking heart, Jude knew his last two scouts and some Mules were gone. How many, he didn't know.

"This way!" the woman called, sensing the group had faltered. "We are almost there!"

A door burst open. Jude and the others stumbled into a large room, rounded and empty, except for flickering torches mounted on large columns. For a few moments they all stood in silence, each recovering from their exertions.

The man and woman smiled at each other. "We knew you would come," the woman said, her face glowing with joy. "Someday, we knew you would come. That thought alone is what has kept us alive all these years."
"Who are you people?" Jude asked.

128

"I am the Baroness Marinetti and this is my husband, the Baron. We own this fortification. It has been in our families for centuries. And now we have become its prisoners."

"But how can you move about so freely if you're prisoners?" asked Jude, the man-of-action.

"The fools!" the Baroness spat. "They forget that we know every inch of this tower, including all the secret passageways. You are quite safe here." The Baron nodded, causing Jude to glance at him.

"They cut out his tongue," the Baroness explained. "...to torture me. After that, I told them enough to leave us alone. But," she added proudly, "Not all. I did not tell them everything." She laughed and gestured to the room.

"We are at the very center of the tower," she explained. "The columns with these torches attached are what hold this entire structure up."

Jude nodded his understanding, surveying his men. There were nine—four more than the job required. "Baroness," he asked. "Is there another way out of this place?"

129

The Baroness shook her head. "Alas, no." She glanced at her husband and he took her hand. "But we are willing to die. Those monsters must be stopped. We are all too well aware of the importance of this Tower. Destroying it will cripple and finish them."

Jude studied the woman. "You've been spying on them, haven't you?"

She nodded.

"How long?"

"Since the beginning. We initially allowed them to set up headquarters here, assuming they meant well. We, too, were fools, Captain."

Jude nodded, thinking.

"Hurry!" said the woman. "Destroy the tower. It's the only way."

"We're going to get you out of here." Jude predicted.

"Impossible!" said the woman.

"Perhaps," he replied, "but it won't stop us from trying. Both of you know things that are very valuable. It will help us."

130

Jude examined his men. "I need two volunteers."

Immediately two stepped forward. He offered his plan. The couple gasped. "Our lives aren't worth all of this!" said the Baroness.

Jude looked sternly at them. "I will be the judge of that."

He gestured to the remaining men as they instantly began to unpack their explosives attaching them to the support columns. "We've got ten minutes, Sir," a Mule said.

"We're going, then," said Jude. He stood at attention, saluting the group. "It has been an honor. After you get it all set up, do your best to get out. Follow the sounds."

They nodded his sentiments and returned to their jobs.

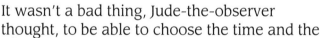

It wasn't a bad thing, Jude-the-observer thought, to be able to choose the time and the way to die. In fact, it made him feel rather powerful.

From where he lay broken and torn, with diminishing sight, Jude was able to watch the Baron and Baroness, swathed in blankets, being checked out by a medic.

131

XVII

The Star

Chapter 14 ...The Star

"Hush. All is well." She repeated. "Rest now."

Jude slept.

"I can't stay long," he said.

"Stay as long as you like," she said. "Take as long as you need."

"There's so much to do," he answered.

"It can wait until you're refreshed," she told him.

Jude breathed in the scent of roses and fell to sleep listening to the delicate sounds of water flowing into the pool.

He awoke, feeling the sun on his face, its warmth on his body.

"How are you feeling now?" she asked.

"Better, thank you."

She gave him cool water to drink.

Jude relaxed, sinking into the moss that was his bed. He slept.

"I have many things to accomplish," he said.

"Are you refreshed?" she asked.

Jude sighed.

She gave him a nourishing broth made with spring vegetables.

She glanced at him. "Shall we become one?" she asked quietly.

Jude quickened.

"Come," she said in reply to his nod and smiled, taking his hand and leading him into the small cottage.

Afterwards, he watched the moon through the

blossoms while he drifted off into sleep.

"I know what to do now," he said. He looked at her. "And I know how to return to you when I've finished."

She smiled.

Jude rose to leave and bowed to her.
"I thank you," he said quietly, drinking in her peaceful beauty.

She tilted her head, acknowledging him.

He exited the small cottage, that final image of her shining in his memory.

Chapter 15 ...The Hermit

Jude had no idea how long he had been sitting, staring off into the distance deep within his thoughts. The fire crackled and burned, encircling him with its warmth. How long had he been watching the little light, swinging to and fro, getting closer and closer?

He straightened, turning his attention fully toward the light. Flashlight? Scanning from side to side to light the trail? Maybe. Coleman lantern? Not bright enough. Flashlight then. Held by whom?   Why travel so late at night? Any good backpacker knew that the camp had to be set and bear proofed by this time of night. Was there an emergency then? Should he be ready to help and dig out his first aid kit? All were questions that flooded his mind.

137

The little swinging light kept getting closer, until finally Jude was able to make out the faint outlines of the traveler who was carrying it—now, he could see that it was a lantern! But not a modern, propane one. It was an old, antique kerosene lantern, quietly flickering in front of its bearer. It blended in with the flicker of his own campfire as the traveler slowed to a stop along the trail.

"Ho!" said the traveler. "Yer still up! Mind the company of an old man who's gotten a bit tired?"

Jude squinted through the flicker of the lantern's light and into the bright eyes of the old man standing politely waiting for an invitation.

Jude shrugged, "Sure, pull up a rock."

The old man smiled and turned fully into the firelight. Jude rummaged around, finding an extra campstool among his belongings. He unfolded it and placed it near the fire, motioning to the old man to sit.

The traveler sat with a sigh, placing the pack he had been carrying beside him. He set the lantern on his knee and carefully turned it off.

Glancing up to see Jude watching him, "need to conserve the fuel," he said.

"Beer?" asked Jude.

The traveler exclaimed, "Now that is very kind of you. I haven't had a beer in ages." He set the lantern down by his pack and stretched his legs toward the fire as Jude lifted the lid of the cooler. He pulled out two beers and handed one to his guest. The wanderer nodded his appreciation.

They sat in silence together, sipping beer. The old man gazed peacefully at the fire as Jude covertly studied him. He was medium height, stocky with square hands and twinkling eyes. His patched and faded clothes were well maintained. Removing his hat, Jude noticed a shock of white hair that was unkempt but clean. It looked as though he hadn't shaved for a few days and his beard seemed to be growing in patches. Jude thought that's probably what made him look more grizzled than he really was. He placed him in his late sixties.

"So," Jude said, breaking the silence, "Where are you heading?"

His guest said with a smile, "Home."

"Where's that?" asked Jude.

"A few days hike from here," the old man replied. "I think, so, anyways. It's been a long time."

"Really?" asked Jude, surprised. He always assumed that the backpackers and campers he ran into along the trail were like him— weekend warriors, up from the city, seeking precious moments of peace and calm. "So how long have you been out here?"

The old man sat forward, arms resting on his knees with the beer can held gently in his hands. "A few years, son," he replied. "....maybe five or six, maybe longer. I've lost track of time. Was doing some bush whackin' one time and found a place—a cave—on a ridge that I kinda took a likin' to. At the time, I wasn't feeling too sociable, and so I marked the way back to the cave, outfitted myself and moved in there."

Jude reappraised his visitor. "Why?"

The old man shrugged. "Seemed like a good thing to do at the time. I wasn't understanding the way of the world anymore. Just wanted out. Marriage died, kids grown. All I really

had left was my health and my love
of this fine land."

"Weren't you lonely?"

The man shook his head realistically. "Not
particularly." He glanced at Jude. "So what
year *is* this?"

He barked out a laugh when Jude told him.
"You don't say??" He smiled and shook his
head, eyes twinkling at Jude.
"Well...well...well. That's quite a surprise!
Really didn't think it was that long." He
continued chuckling and Jude caught himself
grinning too. "I expect I'll have some catching
up to do."

"So how come you've decided to return to
civilization?" Jude asked.

The man sat quietly for a few moments, took
a sip of beer and smiled at Jude. "I have some
things to say, if anyone feels like listening," he
replied mildly. "Things I've learned over the
years I've been away."

"Such as?" asked Jude, reaching into his
cooler, producing two more beers.
The old man took a swallow, "Such as there's
a better way to treat each other, a more

natural way." He took another sip. "Sadly, son, we've been brainwashed to believe we need a lot of unnecessary rules, regulations, laws and beliefs, to keep ourselves from causing harm to one another. It's simply not the case, and I thought maybe I should let people in on a little secret."

"What secret?" asked Jude, leaning toward the old man.

The traveler tapped his heart and then his head. "Think with your heart and not your head. Treat all life as your friend and all life becomes your friend. And do not allow another to take away your happiness. No matter what life throws at you, you've always a choice how you're going to deal with it."

Jude scoffed. "Sounds quite New Agey to me."

"New Age," he said thoughtfully. "I remember that term." He nodded. "It's not a bad term. This can be a New Age, if we let it. It can be whatever *Age* we want it to be." He took another sip from his beer. "But, I'm not planning to stand on some soap box wavin' my arms around, trying to convince people of truths that have been around since the beginning of time, truths that they naturally know in their hearts."

"What are you going to do then?"

"I'm just going to 'be,'" the old man replied.
"When I lived in my cave, I went though every
opinion and belief I had carried up there with
me and I challenged every single one until I
knew exactly who I was and what I believed
and why." He smiled suddenly at Jude. It was
a clear smile of pure joy. "I can never lose my
self again because I know the way back to
my self."

"And who are you?" Jude asked.

Without hesitation, he responded.
"I am a man at peace."

Chapter 16
...The Emperor

"That hurt!" exclaimed Jude. "Please!" she commanded, holding her hand out palm upward.

Her maid placed the brush in her hand. Jude began to angrily run it through her mass of unruly dark curls. She glowered in the mirror at the maid who discretely took two steps backward.

The room was silent except for the snapping of electricity that the act of running a brush through hair countless times creates. The movements seemed to soothe Jude. She eventually apologized to the maid for her curt behavior, as the faithful servant knew she would. Jude was generally pleasant and respectful toward those serving her, creating great loyalty among them, while causing envy for those who were not working for her.

But today was different. It was quite understandable why Jude would not be particularly at her best.

"Where's Bethany?" asked Jude. "I cannot do this alone," she added to herself.

As if on cue, Bethany, Jude's nanny since infancy, swept into the room carrying a beautiful chocolate gown with aquamarine gemstones and tiny seed pearls hand stitched into complicated patterns. It was breathtaking and would enhance Jude's beauty, the aquamarine gems mirroring the blue of her eyes. Jude and Bethany had designed this dress to specifically set off all of her attributes. They considered this as important as any warrior's battle gear.

Today, Jude was going to meet her betrothed, who happened to be an emperor, for the very first time.

As with most engagements in powerful societies who kept peace by alliances and agreements, this marriage had been arranged prior to Jude's birth. She hadn't thought much about it because everyone had told her that it would most likely be a marriage-by-proxy and she would never meet her husband more than once or twice in her lifetime.

Their planet, known mainly for its beauty, was small and peaceful. It was so far from any significant inter-dimensional gateways that it held little to attract power struggles or intrigue. Nobody in the Empire had ever paid it much interest, until very recently. It was actually quite by accident that it had attracted any attention at all.

Two years before Jude's birth, Blade Xavier the First—Emperor of the Fourth Quadrant—and his wife, Empress Evangeline, visited Jude's home planet. It was a last minute decision. They spent several days enjoying its peaceful beauty and the delightful entertainments provided by Jude's parents.

It took nearly three days for the Emperor and Empress to realize that, not only was their every request being met, but it appeared their wishes were being anticipated. This puzzled them and they spent some time trying to ascertain how this phenomena could be. What they discovered thrilled them—so much so, that the need for a strong alliance was created. Thus, before they left the planet, an alliance was formed with Jude's parents.

The marriage of their unborn children sealed the agreement.

Now, thirty years later, that same battle cruiser with the Empire's emblem emblazoned on its surface was orbiting Jude's planet and it was carrying the last person Jude wanted to meet—her fiancé.

Bethany handed the gown to the maid who began to prepare it for Jude. She took the brush and began to thoughtfully arrange Jude's hair, discussing what style might be most becoming.

Jude looked deeply into Bethany's wise old eyes. "What has Fate in mind for me, Nurse?" she asked worriedly.

Bethany smiled and patted Jude's shoulder, "We cannot begin to answer that question until you actually meet him."

Jude smiled miserably and nodded. "I am finding it quite difficult to remain calm and centered."

"Understandable," she replied. "Don't forget, Dear One, that we took that into account when we created your gown."

Jude glanced in the mirror at the gown lying

on her bed. The patterns and whirls created by the stitching veritably shimmered with power that offered great comfort to Jude. "I think I would feel better if I put it on now," she suggested.

"You're not scheduled to meet for another two hours."

"I know," Jude replied, "But I need its support." Jude rose allowing her ladies-in-waiting to dress her, arranging the folds of the dress as they progressed. When they were finished, they offered the full standing mirror for her inspection. Before looking, Jude closed her eyes, feeling the patterns interacting with her essence, blending and supporting her. "It works!" she said with delight. "It's keeping me centered as I relax!"

"Ah, good," replied Bethany. "Then there will be no further worries this day."

Jude nodded, eyes still closed, growing more assured. "I am glad that I listened to you, Nurse," she told Bethany. "I have not yet mastered pure Centering without help."

"You are young, child. Have patience with yourself." Bethany smiled proudly at the young woman whom she loved as if she were her own daughter. "Now, just look at yourself. You are stunning!"

Jude slowly opened her eyes and gazed upon her reflection, smiling at what she saw. Cocking her head to one side, she said, "I'll do very nicely, won't I?" and she laughed happily at her own loveliness. "And now, I would like to enjoy this splendid day as we wait for our esteemed guest."

High above the planet circled *The Strong*, the sentient battlc cruiser of the Emperors. She had been in their service for nearly five hundred years, gaining wisdom and value. Emperor Blade Xavier the Second often relied upon the depth of knowledge that *The Strong* so freely gave to its young master.

The ship's communication link chimed within the Emperor's spacious quarters, "Twenty minutes, sir," a voice said. "Your landing craft is being readied."

"Thank you," he replied to the voice. "I'll be there in fifteen." With a thought, Blade switched off the screen where he had been studying the latest reports on Jude and her people. He had been rather disappointed. For all their talk of their excellence in espionage, his ambassadors offered very little knowledge about the hearts and minds of these beings. Blade sensed that something very important was missing if they did not realize their extraordinary nature.

Blade stood and stretched, reached for the black jacket that completed his uniform and began buttoning it up in front of the dressing mirror.

He was a handsome man, tall, golden and flawless, the fitting image of an emperor. Had he not been born that way, his parents would have altered his DNA to make him so. He studied his reflection, ran his hand through his hair, pulled down his cuffs and smoothed his jacket. He left his quarters, heading for the docking station of his private landing craft.

On his way, Blade carefully went over the points he wanted to make. His nervousness usually gave him an edge. Advisers had prompted him, providing him with as much information as they could. They expected him to agree with their reasoning, when relaying their views. But Blade had his own agenda and that solely depended upon Jude, his future Empress.

"I prefer to go alone," he told the pilot when he reached the shuttle. In disbelief, the pilot hesitantly stepped aside.

"Sir," chimed *The Strong*, "it is not a wise decision."

Blade smiled. "I appreciate your concern," he told the ship, "but I relish the company of my own thoughts and my envoy will be waiting when I arrive."

"I do not trust these people, sir," replied *The Strong*. "They are unusual and unknown."

"And one of them is to be my wife," he replied. "Thank you, but I prefer to go about this my way."

"You, too, are unusual, sir," said *The Strong*.

Blade laughed. "Are you developing humor after all this time?" he asked the ship, as he entered the shuttle's cabin and checked the console in preparation.

The Strong did not answer. Blade snorted. They often spoke in a playful manner. The ship found it refreshing. "Prepare for my

152

immediate departure," Blade said.

The shuttle door closed. Pilot and dock workers retreated to safety and the airlocks opened. Blade maneuvered his craft toward the planet.

The ambassadors comprising Blade's envoy were speaking all at once in outrage. He would have found it amusing if their outrage had not been directed at him. Raising his hand for silence, his eyes blazed with dissatisfaction.

"Must I remind you, *sirs*," he stated as the din had subsided enough for him to be heard, "...that you are *my* ambassadors; that this is *my* envoy."

"But with respect, sir," an elder statesman began, "this is not protocol."

"I am fully aware of that," he answered. "Are you assuming that I am my parents?"

Their voices began to rise once more. Again Blade raised his hand to silence them. "Would you air our differences in public, then?" he asked quietly.

153

All eyes turned toward the elderly woman standing quietly in the back of the room. She bowed deeply to Blade and he acknowledged her respect. "If you would follow me, sir?" she asked.

Blade moved through the opening his envoy made for him as they scrambled to get out of the way. He paid no heed to their mutterings.

"Where is she?" he asked when he reached the older woman's side.

"This way, sir," she said. "I will bring you to her."

Blade walked with the woman down a beautiful white hallway, lit with the light from windows high above. His eyes quickly examined the intricate carvings and weavings decorating the walls. "May I ask for your name?" he inquired.

"I am called Bethany," she replied. "I am the Lady Jude's nurse and close confidante."

"Then you know much about her," he remarked.

Bethany smiled. "She trusts me," she said simply.

Blade nodded, thinking. "And how is she today?" he asked.

154

Bethany paused at a doorway and knocked quietly. "You will soon see for yourself," she answered, her hand on the doorknob.

Blade moved to step through, but Bethany held her hand out, touching his sleeve. He looked at her. "I can see you are strong and very clear. You are like a rock in a river, solid and timeless, but a rock that knows the water flowing by is ever changing it. This is a good thing, young Emperor." She smiled with satisfaction and opened the door.

Jude was gazing out of the floor to ceiling windows. In the view, Blade saw the landing pad and his shuttle. *She has been watching me all this time, appraising me*, he thought.

Jude turned and although Blade was young, he was very good at masking his reactions to happenstance. Her dark hair and light eyes, the perfection of her features was disconcerting as he bowed low, while composing himself.

She stood quietly, her thoughts elusive.

"Lady," he began, searching for the right words. "The images that I have of you did not prepare me."

"They never can," she answered. "I, too, am

unprepared." She added.

Their glances locked.

Following an awkward pause, Blade swallowed and looked about.

"Please," said Jude, "forgive my manners. Would you like to sit?"

He sat and watched her move gracefully to a seat across from him.

"Some refreshment?" she asked.

"Something to drink," he said, "...would be lovely, thank you, My Lady."

He watched her pour two glasses from a pitcher of rose-infused water on the small table between them. He took the glass and raised it to his lips abd they drank in unison.

Jude sat back, with a half smile. "I understand that your people are not too pleased with you."

"How?" Blade began, but changed his mind. "...Yes. They think I am young, which I am in years. But they don't know me."

"Ah," she said. "That is an important oversight."

"It is. And one that I do not wish to make with you." He took another sip of water. "I

156

have a proposition for you." He said abruptly. "I have thought of my approach...how to begin...but, having met you, I am unsure."

Jude raised an eyebrow. "The truth is a good place," she said.

"One would think," he replied. "But I do not often find it so in my dealings with men." He continued. "We are a technologically based society. I am aware that you are not, so I want to be clear what that means and how I have been prepared for my role as Emperor, as Leader of this Quadrant."

He paused. Jude nodded and leaned slightly forward, encouraging him to continue.

"Since before my birth, as soon as there was the slightest detection of consciousness, I was indoctrinated with knowledge—data on everything I would possibly need to make conscious decisions and appraisals on any given subject. My brain has been modified and upgraded; enhanced with software to house and sort the knowledge that I have."

Jude was studying him with her head cocked as he spoke. Blade gathered this was something she did often and found he liked it.

"I sometimes feel I have more in common with *The Strong*, my ship, than I do with those I command," he regretfully admitted with a smile.

She smiled back, her warmth encouraging him.

"There has been a change," he said. "And it began with the chance meeting of our parents. My parents have been technologically enhanced as well. My father, and then after marriage, my mother."

At her gasp, Blade paused and held out a hand as if to soothe her. "No, wait, hear me out. I am not suggesting that you be altered. On the contrary!"

Jude centered herself and responded to his concern. "Forgive me," she said simply, "I did not mean to interrupt. I am...," she searched for the right words, "...unlike yourself, I still have much to learn."

Blade relaxed and continued. "When my parents met your parents, they discovered a kingdom without conflict and it baffled them. From an initial glance, your people appeared to be averagely evolved, not yet in the technological age. But, when they began to talk with your people, my parents realized they possessed a knowing of things they could not possibly have knowledge of, even of events that transpired light years away from your own planet."

Blade leaned forward. "But it wasn't just the knowledge your parents possessed. It was their ability to detect truth from falsehood and their willingness to forgive and to please. This desire to please confounded my parents. Originating in a true desire to ease another's burdens, it was a strength, a virtue, not a weakness. It was from choice. Intrigued, they found that their vast data banks of knowledge couldn't disclose any further information."

Blade continued. "As we both are well aware, they formed an alliance with your world and sealed the agreement with our union. I agree with this union, Lady Jude. But I do not agree with my parents' reasoning as to why. Simply put, they wanted to add your DNA to our gene pool."

Blade gauged her reaction to his statement, but her eyes revealed nothing as the silence lengthened. Then she took a deep breath tilted her head, and asked, "And what is your proposal?" She paused before saying, "Your truth throughout this negotiation is greatly appreciated."

Blade blinked. It had not occurred to him that he was in negotiation, even if he had begun the conversation as a "proposal." "That requires a little further explanation," he told her.

Jude agreed, taking a sip of water, watching him with her intelligent eyes.

"I am not my parents. I appreciate all the knowledge that I possess and I appreciate the power and responsibility that I own as a result of my privileged position. I enjoy being an emperor, but I am not my parents.

"Since your people were an enigma to us, I made it a point to study more and," he shrugged his shoulders and grinned, "you are still an enigma to me."

"But that doesn't mean I want to simply combine our DNA. What I've learned is that there are personality traits we've neglected over the centuries. We have lost something that we are unaware of. When I see your treatment of each other, I feel a deep yearning and a feeling of loss. Somehow, somewhere in the past, my people took a wrong turn and decided to ignore humanitarian care. "

Blade became quiet, and in the stillness, Jude could sense his earnestness. "Lady Jude, I wish to truly unite our people in order to have a better empire. I do not wish to conquer. I wish to confer. I wish to blend my strength with your strength." He paused, remembering Bethany's words in describing her relationship with Jude. "I wish to trust you, and I wish for you to trust me."

He took a deep breath, forcing himself to relax. He had not realized how tense he had become. Even augmented, the role of Empress had never been an equal position to that of Emperor. If Jude were to agree and accept his proposal, he would be changing history. And, he would be giving up his control on a hunch, a yearning, and a feeling.

Looking at Jude, Blade again saw a momentary unfocusing and refocusing of her vision as if her very consciousness left her body. Then she looked at him and smiled so genuinely pure, that it hurt.

"I think," she said, "We have something to work with, here."

VIII

Strength

Chapter 17 ...Strength

Jude ducked down the alley that ran next to the dojo or martial arts school where he trained, his gear bag draped over one shoulder.

"There he goes!" came a shout from behind and Jude snorted in disgust.

Disappearing into the shadows underneath a fire escape, he waited for the four familiar figures to run noisily by. He quietly slipped back out of the alley, changing directions and merged with the foot traffic, arriving at his home without incident.

It all had begun with an article that his girlfriend had written about him for the school newspaper. If his girlfriend hadn't been so popular, and if he hadn't been such a computer geek, complete with glasses taped with adhesive tape, the article would have been forgotten in a week.

But, no.... It had gone all *Karate Kid* on him. Four of the high school jocks (one of them, Brian, a linebacker and his girlfriend's ex) decided he needed a lesson, and had begun stalking him. They discovered his class schedule and could be found lurking in the hallways outside his classes, taunting him and goading him into a confrontation.

Jude wondered how they were doing with their own education, if they were spending so much time following him around. He also wondered why teachers were turning a blind eye to the whole deal. But, maybe they thought, as he had once thought, that it was all going to blow over.

Unfortunately, the article had been published almost three weeks ago, and the neanderthals were showing no signs of stopping. And he was really beginning to be annoyed. In fact, they were starting to show up at places outside of school. So far, Jude had been able to either ignore or avoid them, but he knew, if they didn't give up, that some sort of confrontation was inevitable.

Thinking more about it, Jude flipped on the light in his bedroom. He pulled out his white gi top, the uniform he worked out in, from his gear bag and slung it on a chair to dry. He thought it probably should be washed but he didn't feel like it at the moment. Instead, he stretched out on his bed, leaning against the headboard and pondering the four bullies looking for a fight.

Jude had no doubt that he could take them. After all, he *was* a second degree black belt and knew a thing or two about jujitsu. But fighting was never the answer. He had learned that lesson at his very first class when he was five. His sensei always taught that you don't learn martial arts to fight. Rather, you learned them so you wouldn't have to fight. It was all about control and discipline.

Then there were the boneheads who thought everything had to be settled with a punch. He called it the Thug Mentality. Sure, he was a guy, he got mad as hell, and he would have loved teaching those guys a lesson they'd never forget. But, Jude liked problem solving better. He loved to use his mind to outwit his opponents. It was why martial arts was such a perfect fit. He enjoyed following the energy flow of techniques, the structure of the body and how it all worked together in time and space. He loved how he could anticipate his adversary's movement based on how they were standing or looking. Better still, he loved the psychology of getting a nemesis to behave the way he wanted them, to defeat them from within. To Jude, martial arts was physical chess.

So usually, dealing with these four should be easy, Jude thought. But these guys had gotten the better of him. It suddenly dawned on him that by being angry and annoyed at the four, they were actually defeating *him* from within without even realizing it. But Jude did, and it was time for for him to put a stop to it.

Jude had learned that the best way to successfully resolve conflict is to go in without a plan, stay centered, and live in the moment. He decided it was time to take charge of the wacky weirdness.

The eventual outcome surprised even him.

The bell for the end of the day sounded and Jude gathered his stuff together from the computer lab and got ready for jujitsu. It was his day to help teach the younger ones.

166

"What a surprise," he said as he left the lab, "my entourage."

The four punks immediately started to heckle him as he headed for the exit. In the middle of a stride, Jude turned abruptly and stopped in a ready stance, staring directly into the eyes of each of his antagonists, studying them. He realized that they were just...boys—boys with a pack mentality because they didn't really know how to become their own true selves. He actually felt sorry for them and it surprised him.

"How did I get so lucky?" he said out loud. He wasn't referring to them, even though they thought so. He was thinking about how he could have been one of them and he was grateful he didn't turn out that way.

Brian, the linebacker, reached out to push Jude, but he easily deflected him. "Shhhhh!" he ordered. "I'm thinking."

"Huh?" asked Brian.

"Quiet," replied Jude. "I'm figuring out something."

"What a bunch of BS!" Brian scoffed and took a swing. Jude quickly parried and suddenly the larger boy found himself in an arm lock, eyes widening in surprise. "Owww! Leggo!"

167

The other three blinked. It had happened too fast for them to react.

"I've got an idea," Jude offered, keeping tension on Brian so that whenever he struggled he winced.

Two of the other boys made a simultaneous grab for Jude, but he kept Brian between them, as he kept moving down toward the exit door. He was flowing with their combined energies. He was beginning to have fun.

At the door, he wheeled to face the three, bringing Brian to his knees. "Crap!" cried Brian, "that hurts!"

"Okay," Jude said, ignoring Brian's pleas. "I'll fight you guys if that's what you want."

All three then tried to rush him, but Brian was in between and got the brunt of their efforts. "Stop it, you idiots!" shouted Brian through clenched teeth. "Back off until he at least lets me go. Crap!"

The three hesitated.

"On one condition," continued Jude conversationally.

"What's that, wimp?" asked one of the others.

168

"You take us one at a time?"

"And spoil my fun? Not hardly!" He replied.
"No, I want you all to watch me teach
classes tonight."

"And why would we do that?" sneered another.

"Because I'd rather recruit you than fight you,"
Jude told them.

"You gotta be kiddin' me! Owww!" Brain
insisted, still in an arm lock, still on his knees.
"You want to recruit us? Why?"

"Why not? You guys stick together, you're
persistent, you're loyal. Those are good
qualities for a martial artist to possess. Good
raw material."

They were speechless.

A crowd was beginning to form. "Guys, I'm
looking like a dork, here." Brian said. "Let's
do it so he'll let me up." The others nodded.

"Okay then," releasing Brian, Jude continued,
"I've got a car. Let's go."

The other boys rushed to help Brian up, but he
shook them off and dusted his knees. "He
was just showing us some of his stuff," he told
the crowd. "We're thinking about joining."

"Gotta run," Jude realized. "I'm late."

"You heard him," Brian said. "Let's do this."

Later that evening, Jude glanced over at his "entourage" sitting on the benches reserved for parents and onlookers, while focusing on the class being taught. With each class, the ages increased and the techniques became more refined and more difficult. The last class, Jude's class, was taught by the sensei, or teacher, and consisted of the two highest ranks; the brown belts and the black belts. The sensei used him as his assistant, to demonstrate the different techniques. (Jude always thought being sensei's assistant was a lot like being a crash test dummy). At the end of the class, after he had bowed off the mat, he went over to the four.

"Still want to fight?" he asked, mopping his face with a cloth he kept in his gi.

Brian laughed. "We liked that last class when your teacher was throwing you around. Some of that stuff looked like it hurt."

"To tell the truth, it doesn't feel that great."

"Looks like you got beat up enough. We're happy."

170

"So what did you think?"

Brian looked at the others. "We were thinkin' we might like to try it out." They nodded in agreement.

Jude smiled. "I'm glad. It's a lot of fun, but also a lot of hard work. My sensei, Sandy," he nodded at a young black belt, a girl from another high school, "and I will be putting you through the paces."

"We figured, if you could do it, so could we," joked Brian.

Jude grinned and called over the sensei to introduce him to the four new recruits. Watching their enthusiasm and hearing their excited questions, Jude realized that he was actually looking forward to getting to know them better.

It surprised the heck out of him.

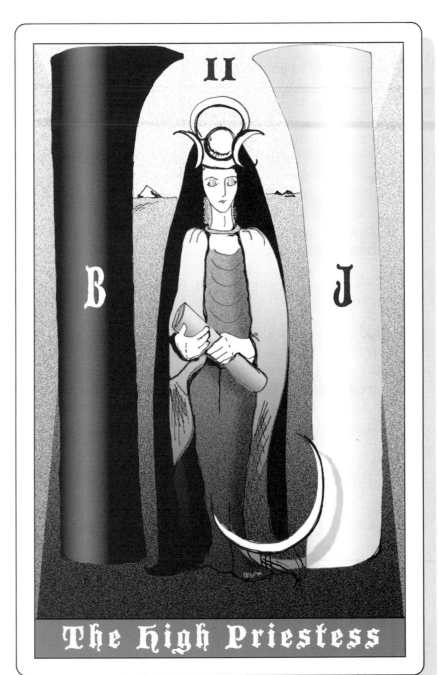

The High Priestess

Chapter 18
...The High Priestess

"There I go again," Jude thought to herself, "not keeping my mouth shut and now regretting it." She picked up a stone from the sand and hurled it into the waves, watching as it was swallowed by the surf. She threw several more and with a sigh, continued to walk along the deserted beach, feeling the waves tug at her feet.

Normally, a simple walk on the beach was all she needed to regain her high spirits, but not today. She just couldn't get the conversation she had with her father out of her mind. All she wanted was for him to appreciate her point of view and the fact that he never listened made her so frustrated and angry! Trying to get her point across was like shouting at a bank vault to open after hours.

She really *did* want him to understand her, and be proud of her.

"Why doesn't he hear me?" she shouted to the wind. A lone gull glanced down, making its mournful cry in response. "He never even tries to see things from my perspective." She whispered with a sigh, "Ever."

Walking along in silence, she ignored the fact it could rain any minute. Instead, she allowed the biting wind to continue to push her, while the waves were splashed on her legs, sea foam blowing by. It mirrored her mood, she mused as she carefully went over their latest argument.

Jude had left her job at her father's design firm a year ago, and had accepted another position at a smaller, less established one. This new position gave her full control of the art department, which was in fact, just herself. The small design firm had nearly doubled its client base with her on board and she was overjoyed at her contribution. She loved her new job.

It had not been a sudden or easy decision for her. While with her father's firm, Jude had tried desperately to get ahead. When she was first hired right out of school, he told her he was not going to show her any favoritism. She agreed and told him she didn't want any, instead being allowed to earn her own advancement. She had been surprised by the fact that he had hurt, embarrassed and finally, angered her by his cruel treatment. His remarks were so demeaning that she concluded that he was overcompensating so that no one could accuse him of partiality. The sympathetic gazes she constantly received from her co-workers was more than she could bear. She knew it was time to leave before she grew to despise her father. When the opportunity finally arose, she jumped on it.

With the knowledge that her father would be hurt, she had written a long letter explaining herself and her reasons. He simply handed it back to her, without even reading it. Their relationship deteriorated even further after that incident. At family occasions, he treated her with civility, but the warmth was gone. She had never been able to find a private moment with him to explain. Her siblings only told her it was her problem, when she asked them to step in. When she asked her mother about it, she was told to "just give your father time."

Jude felt that a year was "time" enough. So when she knew her father would be home, she drove over to have a talk with him in anticipation of clearing the air. It was a total disaster. It concluded with her running from the house in tears of frustration and sorrow, and winding up at the ocean.

While watching the graceful curves of a line of pelicans as they skimmed over the surface of the waves, Jude slowed. She wiped a tear from her cheek and brushed her thick, curly hair off of her face. Seeing a huge log half buried in sand, she sat with a sigh.

Her father had originally brought her to this beach, and she recalled that day well. They both loved finding places of solitude and then sharing them with each other. Agreeing that this beach was a rare find, they both had rated it a "ten."

Exasperated, Jude cried out loud, "I don't know what to do anymore! I'm so tired of trying."

Those are the wisest words you have said upon the subject.

Jude jumped, startled, and looked around. The only things in sight were the ocean, beach and shore birds. She was alone.

In surrendering your control of the outcome,

176

you have allowed infinite possibilities to resolve this conflict.

Jude swallowed. "Who are you?"

When you surrender your control of the outcome, you open yourself to you inner wisdom.

"Are you my inner wisdom?" Jude asked, her curiosity overriding her fears.

You can call me that.

"Why haven't I heard you before?"

But you have. You listen to me all the time. I have guided you throughout your lifetime. Whenever you received clarity on your decisions, you had been talking with me.

"But not like *this*!" Jude claimed. "I've never heard a voice in my head like I'm going crazy or something."

Perhaps this situation called for an inner dialogue. The voice sounded amused. *You are not crazy, I assure you. Think of all the times you hold inner dialogues with people—when you rehearse your proposals, for example. This time, you are having an inner dialogue with yourself, with that part of you which is tapped into universal wisdom.*

177

"Okaaaayyy," said Jude, skeptically, "so what does my Inner Wisdom want to say about me and my dad?"

To make a decision that gives you the most relief. I felt your relief when you gave up. That is the right thing to do.

"I still feel sad," said Jude. "And angry."

Because you are thinking about it again. When you said that you were tired of trying, you let go of the situation and then what did you feel?

"Relief!" replied Jude, surprised.

Exactly. You gave up, which is another word for "surrender" and you allowed solutions to unfold. You changed the way you thought about the situation and, therefore, the outcome will change.

"For the better?" asked Jude.

A positive person like yourself who always is looking for the good in life? Without a doubt.

For several minutes, Jude sat in silence, allowing the ocean to relax her. "I do feel better," she thought. "I feel hopeful and it feels good."

Jude heard footsteps in the sand and looked

178

up to see an approaching figure.

"I thought I might find you here," her father explained, gesturing to the log she was sitting on, "May I?"

Jude made room for him. They sat in silence, two people so very much alike, watching and absorbing the sounds of the surf.

"I've missed you," her father finally admitted.

Jude leaned her head on his shoulder. "I missed you, too, Daddy."

The High Priest

Chapter 19
...The High Priest

Jude lay flat on his belly, his fists supporting his chin. The sun was shining on his back as he imagined what it would be like to be one of the seeds in the field that spread out before him, buried deep in the ground and feeling the sun slowly reaching him.

A shadow crossed the scene, causing him to look up. He half rolled over, one muddy hand pushing the thick mass of dark curls out of his eyes. A streak appeared on his cheek from his hand.

Jude's older brother with an old man leaning on his arm came into view. They paused, and his brother scoffed at his appearance. The old man smiled, saying simply, "Tonight."

Jude's eyes widened. How could Grandfather

possibly know what he was thinking? How could he know that Jude was wondering when he would be able to see the baby plants pushing through the soil?

"That's what I would be wondering," said Jude's grandfather, the High Priest.

Jude's jaw dropped in awe as the old man chuckled. His laughter faded as Jude's brother helped their grandfather toward the temple. Jude watched them for awhile, then returned to watching the seeds.

He imagined they were growing. The seeds had been planted in the field a few days ago; it had rained and now the sun was shining. If he were a seed, he would want to grow and look around.

His neck began to get sore, so he laid his cheek down on the rich soil. He closed his eyes, and began the Feeling Game. He felt the sun on his back, his bare legs and on his outstretched arms. His fingers dug into the earth and felt the dirt crumble, making room for his fingers. He felt the warm sun on one cheek and he felt the cool earth on the other. He could feel the fresh breeze on the backs of his knees, and a fly land on one calf. It tickled and he twitched it off.

He fell asleep and dozed until he felt his brother kick the bottom of his foot. On his way back from escorting their grandfather to the temple, his brother paused to sneer, "You are so stupid. An idiot in the making, if ever there was one." His brother moved on, leaving a wake of hurt and sadness.

As if whispering to him like a mother, a breeze tickled his ears, "Hush, now," it gently soothed. Jude sighed and resumed the Feeling Game, adding the Listening Game as well.

He then flipped over, opening his eyes and began the Feeling, Listening and added a third, the Seeing game.

Later that night, the moonlight swept across the sleeping room, eventually reaching Jude, who was curled silently in a pallet next to his brother. His eyes blinked open and he was momentarily dazzled by the brightness. *Why am I awake?* Finally remembering, he scrambled for his clothes and dressed quietly. Rolling over his brother who grumbled in his sleep, Jude tiptoed out of the sleeping room. He headed toward the field he had been to that morning. No one saw him leave, except for one bright, twinkling eye belonging to an old, wise man. In a few moments, he got up and followed.

"Grandfather?" Jude's brother asked, awakened instantly by the rustling of the old man. "Are you in need of help?"

"Hush, boy," the high priest replied gently, "I am well, go back to sleep."

Jude was awestruck by the beauty of the night. The moon painted the fields silver, effecting a magical quality to the landscape. Illuminating the night so much that there was no need of any further lighting, the boy flew through the little town. In no time he was flopped once again on his belly, with his chin resting on his fists, absorbed in watching for signs of growth amidst the furrows of that very same field.

With a small gasp, a little smile curved his lips. Squinting hard, Jude watched a dirt clod roll down the side of one of the furrows, about twelve inches from his nose. Suddenly, a tiny pale sprout appeared. Another clump of dirt rolled and, a tiny sprout appeared. As he continued to watch with wide eyes, he saw more and more of them. A laugh began to build deep within him. It burst forth excitedly as he watched the magic of the seeds.

"Hello!" he quietly called to the sprouts, and he felt them answering. "Why are you growing at night?" he asked them.

He heard them all reply with one voice. "We pulled energy from the warmth of the sun and the earth, but only in the deep night can we begin our journey," they told him.

"Why?" he asked.

"Because the darkness allows us to focus only on our growing," they responded.

Jude was quiet, watching them.

"You grow well," he told them.

"Thank you," they replied, "we know. As do you."

Jude rested his head on his arms and looked up at the moon. "I don't know that I am growing or not," he sighed. "I can't tell."

"That's because you are doing it. You have to rely on others to tell you," answered a voice from above.

Jude gasped and scrambled to his feet, looking up at the old, wise face of his grandfather. "Grandfather! Are you okay?" he asked reaching out to steady the gentleman.

His grandfather chuckled, waving off the offer of assistance and gestured at the cane he was leaning on. "I am fine, boy. Like you, I was hoping to greet our crops."

Jude looked back at the seedlings. "You were right, Grandfather! It was tonight. How did you know?"

"I could hear their singing, and it was growing louder."

"What do you mean, their singing?" Jude asked.

"All things have a song, my boy. All things are expressing the One Consciousness in their own, unique way. That is the song they sing, their unique song. A wise man listens and learns to interpret the songs."

They stood in silence and Jude strained his ears. "I can't hear them, Grandfather."

"Are you trying to hear them with your ears?"

"Yes, as hard as I can."

"Ah, well then," his grandfather replied, "That is your mistake. You can't hear them with your ears. You must hear the songs with your heart."

"My heart? Grandfather, that's silly!" Jude giggled.

"Were you not talking to the plants earlier?"

Jude became still, looking up at his grandfather. "I was."

"How were you hearing their answer? With your ears?"

Jude exclaimed. "No, I wasn't! I didn't even know that I wasn't! How can that be?"

"Because you were using your heart to hear them. Now, try that when listening for their song."

Jude focused. He recalled the joy and wonder he felt when he first saw the tiny sprouts pushing through the soil. He concentrated on those feelings. From there, he began to listen. The beauty of their song flowed through him so strongly that his knees buckled and he sat right down where he had been standing.

His grandfather smiled, as he watched the boy's face transform into pure joy. "They will sing a different song when their seed has ripened," he told Jude. "That's how I know when to proclaim Harvest Day."

Jude was silent, listening to the song of the wheat. "I don't know where I end and where

187

the seeds begin. I feel I will break into a million pieces. How can you stand it, Grandfather?"

"By listening to your own song. That is the most important song to know. By knowing your own song, you remain whole. It will always call you home from the journeys of your mind and soul."

Jude turned his focus on himself and listened to his own song. A tear unknowingly slid down his cheek. "I am home, Grandfather," he announced. "I am beautiful."

His grandfather spoke gently, "You are indeed, my boy. Come. It is late and tomorrow is a big day. Off to bed with us." He held out his hand and helped the boy to stand.

"Grandfather! You're strong!" Jude declared.

Laughing, the patriarch stated, "Of course I am, Jude! I may be old and unsteady but I am still strong." He sobered and looked at Jude thoughtfully, drawing the boy's attention to his next words. "Tonight you have proven to me what I have guessed long ago."

"What is that, Grandfather?"

"Because you can hear the Songs of Life, you

will be the next High Priest. Tomorrow, we begin."

Jude grimaced.

"But, why would you frown?" asked the old man. "This is a great gift."

"I don't want to be led all 'round by my brother!" the boy wailed.

The High Priest laughed.

Chapter 20
...The Hanged Man

Jude parked her bicycle by the library, put the backpack on her shoulder and wandered over to the Green. It was a warm summer day and with a fresh breeze off the lake, much of the humidity was gone. The freshness of the day caused her to think of the approaching fall and back to school. She frowned slightly. School was okay, but nothing like summer vacation. She didn't know if she was ready to be a senior yet. She knew she would like the freedom it would bring, but the next step would be choosing college and her life would change—big time. She would also have to go back to work. She realized she ought to be grateful that her parents had given her the summer off, while many of her friends were working at the local Dairy Queen, because it allowed her time to relax and write, which was her passion.

Locating an accommodating tree, Jude sat down and leaned against its trunk. She pulled her current book from her backpack and settled in for an hour or two of reading as she waited for her friends. This had been her routine for most of the summer and by sitting on the Green, eventually somebody she knew would show up.

About a half hour into her book, Jude looked up to rest her eyes. She saw her friend Shauna coasting her bike toward the bike rack by the library. She glanced over in Jude's direction. Jude briefly waved before returning to her reading. She was reaching the end of a chapter and wanted to finish before Shauna arrived.

"Hey," Shauna said as she approached.

"Hey yourself," Jude replied, closing her book. "How are you?"

"Good to great. You?"

Jude smiled. "Same." She put her book back into to her pack and stood, stretching. "Have anything in mind?"

Shauna shrugged, "Not really, I was thinking about kicking around by the lake."

"Sounds good." Jude agreed.

The two friends began heading toward the lake, pausing occasionally to look in their favorite store windows.

Finally, Jude remarked, "This is such a cool town."

"I know, the fact that we live in a vacation spot. It's like, we've already begun our vacation while the rest are just getting here," Shauna said, nodding.

"Yeah, and they have to leave, but we get to keep living here when the season ends," Jude added, "Sometimes there's a lot of people and it's really busy and other times, it's just *us locals*."

In awhile Jude commented, "I like checking out all the tourists."

"Yeah, like him!" Shauna pointed to a man, obviously lost. "How can anybody get lost in this tiny town?"

They both laughed and approached the man. He was grateful when they helped him find the rental boat dock.

Reaching a sandy beach on the shore near the

boardwalk, the two settled down to enjoy the sun where they could see other friends that might be around. Jude leaned against her backpack and stretched out her legs, sighing contentedly.

"Have you heard about the party over at Graham's tonight? His parents will be out of town." Shauna told her.

"Cool," she replied, adding, "I wonder how come it's more fun when parents are gone. It's not like we do anything differently."

Shauna shrugged. "I dunno. Probably because then we don't feel like we're being watched."

She continued to drone on about the people they knew and who said what to whom. It was nothing new to Jude and she began to lose interest, finding herself lulled by wavelets lapping on the shore and the gentle sway of the boats against the dock. The air felt fresh and clean while Shauna's voice was reduced to a distant hum.

"Oh, God!" exclaimed Shauna, startling Jude out of her trance, "The Village Idiot!"

Jude looked over at her friend who was watching a distant figure on the sand. She squinted. "Who are you talking about?"

"Mark Bastion! And he's heading this way. Jude, I seriously don't want to deal with that guy. He's way too weird." She bounced to her feet, gathered her things, and hinted to Jude. "Are you comin' with me?"

Jude yawned. "No. I'm too comfortable here and I'm not letting anyone take that away from me."

"Suit yourself. See you tonight." With that, Shauna was off.

Jude nodded to her friend and watched as she disappeared from view. She turned her attention to the approaching figure, Mark Bastion. She had never had a problem with him. He was different, but he wasn't an idiot. Chances are, he was probably smarter than Shauna and all their friends combined. Anyway, Jude thought he was kind of cute in a different sort of way. He never tried to be like anyone he wasn't. She liked how his hair flopped into his mesmerizing eyes. Whenever he looked at her, she felt as though he was seeing all of her, not just her face, but her thoughts and feelings too.

Jude's and Mark's parents were friends. So, even though he was a couple of years older they played together in her early childhood. It wasn't until she was a little older that his quirkiness began to make her slightly uncomfortable. In high school, she didn't want to be associated with him because he didn't fit in with her group, and she had tried to avoid him. But he was in college now and she didn't even know he was back.

Suddenly, Jude realized that Mark wasn't coming over to her after all, and she snickered thinking about how fast Shauna had left the beach. Knowing Mark, he most likely didn't even realize that they were there. She settled back to watch him.

The beach was curved, creating a larger patch of sand where an old jungle gym and swing set had been put up. She remembered spending many happy hours swinging and climbing with Mark and others. He quickly arrived at the monkey bars and was soon hanging upside down. Jude's brow furrowed as she watched him swing. Soon, everything in his pants pockets was persuaded by gravity to fall to the sand. It seemed that Mark hadn't even noticed. Jude smirked, turning her attention back to the dock, the boats and the lake's horizon.

However, she couldn't relax like earlier.

Despite how hard she tried, her attention was drawn back to Mark swinging on the monkey bars. A small group of children had gathered around the jungle gym, as if they weren't quite sure if they should play there while a grown up was hanging upside down. It tickled Jude to watch their indecision. Mark seemed to make all ages wonder.

The gang of kids grew tired and wandered over to the swings, while Mark continued hanging. Jude pulled out her book and tried to read. But she kept looking over at Mark. With a sigh, she clapped the book shut and shoved it back into her pack. She got up, swinging her pack over one shoulder and headed over to the jungle gym.

Her sandals crunched to a halt in the coarse sand under the monkey bars.

"What exactly are you doing?" she inquired.

"I'm changing my mind," he replied.

"What do you mean, you're changing your mind?" Jude asked.

Mark shrugged. At least she thought it was a shrug—after all, it was upside down. "I thought if I changed my perspective on the world, my opinions would change as well.

I thought that hanging upside down would be a way of physically altering my perspective." Jude started picking up the things that had fallen out of his pockets, thinking about his answer. "Why?" she asked finally.

Mark took a breath. "Last semester, I was studying the mythologist, Joseph Campbell, and he says to *'follow your bliss.'* I liked that. The problem is, I really have no idea what my bliss is or how to follow it. I know a lot about other people's ideas of what *my bliss* should be, but I want to know what mine actually is so I can follow it. I've been thinking about it so much and just going in mental circles, that I needed to see it all differently. I wanted to erase all of my previous perceptions and start fresh. Hanging upside down seemed like a good place to start."

"Well, is it? You're face is pretty red."

"It should be by now. I feel terrible." He took a deep breath. "My head feels like it will burst and my legs and hands have gone numb."

Jude tried, in vain, to suppress a laugh. "I'm sorry!" she said, " I don't mean to laugh at you. I just can't help it! Sometimes you're just too much, Mark. Do you want me to help you get down?"

"Yes, please," he said. "I'm not sure if I can get down by myself right now." He squinted up at her. "That *is* you, Jude, right?"

"Who else could it possibly be?" she asked as she supported his back to allow him to untangle himself. She helped him pry one leg from the bar to get him going but he landed in a heap at her feet anyway.

"Ooof!"

"Are you okay?" She kneeled beside him, helping him sit up.

He looked at her as if in a daze while trying to refocus. "Whoa," he said, putting a hand to his head. "Don't ever do that for very long."

Jude burst out laughing again. "Your things," she said, handing him the items from his pockets. He nodded in thanks, stuffing them back into his pockets. He smiled at her crookedly.

"I bet that looked pretty bizarre, huh?" he asked.

"Of course it did, but not any more than usual. How did it work?"

"How did what work?"

"Were you able to change your mind?"

Mark stood, balancing unsteadily before helping her to her feet. "I'll let you know in a minute," he reported.

He headed for the shoreline. Jude picked up her pack and followed. The kids that had moved to the swings returned to the monkey bars and began hanging upside down.

Jude stood next to Mark who stood in silence looking at the vague outline of the other shore. As his silence lengthened, she glanced at Mark, with his floppy hair, standing tall and upright with his hands in his pockets. He noticed and smiled.

"I did find my bliss." He finally said.

"So, what is it?"

"I'm going to follow new ideas to see where they'll take me. Whatever it is that makes me curious."

Jude questioned. "But, can you major in that and make a living that way?"

Mark shrugged. "I don't know. But it feels..." he hesitated, "*right.* I have never thought about this before. There's always been a plan for everything. I've always carefully mapped it out so I wouldn't get lost...like my life was this big chemistry experiment or something. But this…is so new. " He looked over at her and chuckled, "I think I'll need to sort this one out. It's so strange…."

They were silent for a while.

"What are you doing tonight?" Mark asked abruptly.

"I was thinking of going to a party," Jude shrugged, "But, I'm not sure. You?"

"Would you like to come over to my house to get caught up on things?"

Jude thought for a second, and said. "Sure, why not?"

"You won't change your mind?" he asked with concern. "I know I don't really belong in your crowd. I remember what it was like in high school."

She looked back at the row of kids still hanging upside down on the monkey bars and grinned at the sight. "I'm not really sure who 'my crowd' is any more," she answered.

Chapter...The Sun 21

Jude looked up from his writing, re-focusing on the world around him, noticing his butt ached from sitting too long on the park bench. It was the sound of a child's laughter that had pulled him from his work.

His child.

His wife was wearing her "God-I'm-so-late" expression as she ran across the street. Reaching the other side, she saw Jude. Her expression changed. She kept running.

Jude set aside his laptop and rose.

His fifteen-month-old son was cuddled close in his wife's arms, being jostled up and down with each hurried step. His head was flopping back and forth, arms stretched wide, eyes closed in abandonment and joy. Pure pleasure. Bliss.

He had his mother's blond hair and blue eyes. His unruly curls—tossed by the breeze—were pure Jude.

His laugh—his golden, warm laugh—was all his own.

As Above, So Below

Darkness, and Then Light

Light, and Then Darkness

So It Has Always Been

Maybe It's Time For a Change

206

A BRIEF EXPLANATION OF THE TAROT'S MAJOR ARCANA CARDS

0 *The Fool*—Innocence. Faith. New beginning of a cycle. Trusting in synchronicity.

1 *The Magician*—Creation. Magic. Self-Mastery. Creative control over all four elements.

2 *The High Priestess*—Inner Wisdom. Intuition.

3 *The Empress*—Queen. Earth Mother. Nurturer. Cycles of creation and destruction.

4 *The Emperor*—Authority with integrity. Power with compassion. Leadership. Form and structure.

5 *The High Priest (Hierophant)*— Knowledge. Guidance. Traditional wisdom. Learn through challenging your beliefs.

6 *The Lovers*—Balance and union. Blending of two natures to form a third. Choosing between fantasy and reality, between sacred and profane.

7 *The Chariot*—Triumph.
Using mental focus to create
movement and change.

8 *Strength*—Mastery of fear through
love and understanding. Turning
adversary into ally through
acceptance. Conquering with love.

9 *The Hermit*—Wisdom born from
deep soul searching and
quiet introspection.

10 *The Wheel*—The natural cycle of
life. The moment when a new
cycle begins.

11 *Justice*—Balance. Reaping
what you have sown, cause
and effect.

12 *The Hanged Man*—Surrendering to
the process. Looking at life from a
new perspective. A time of waiting.

13 *Death*—Letting go of that which is
no longer working, making room for
rebirth, renewal. Getting down to
the bones.

14 *Temperance*—Alchemy. Synthesis.
Allowing. Flow. Enduring the
intense and occasionally painful
process of personal tempering,
or transformation.

15 *The Devil*—Self-imprisonment created by negative thought forms and fearful beliefs.

16 *The Tower*—Radical and sudden destruction of that which obstructs freedom and self-realization.

17 *The Star*—Enlightenment. Peace. Potential becoming actuality. Oneness with All That Is.

18 *The Moon*—Mystery. Change. Digging deep into your subconscious and making friends with your shadow self.

19 *The Sun*—Enthusiasm. Joy. Delight in creative play. Wholeness, balance of masculine and feminine, anima and animus.

20 *Judgment*—Transformation. Freedom. Heeding the call to wake up and become your Full Self.

21 *The Universe (World)*—Completion. Celebration of a Journey whose souvenirs are knowledge, wisdom and inner joy.

ABOUT THE AUTHOR

Cynthia Campbell Williams lives on five acres in the Northern Californian Redwoods with her husband, son, two dogs, five cats and all the wild things that share their space with her.

She is an oil painter, a writer, a Soul Memory Discovery Facilitator and Certified Life Coach.

Please feel free to contact her at:
Cammy@CampbellShepardWilliams.com

or visit her two websites:
www.CampbellShepardWilliams.com
www.InJoyandGrace.com